THE DREAM TRAVELER'S
Game
OUT OF THE DARKNESS

THE DREAM TRAVELER'S SERIES
——— BOOK 7 ———

TED DEKKER & H.R. HUTZEL

ISBN 979-8-9888509-0-8 (Paperback Edition)

Also available in the Dream Travelers Game series

The Boy and his Song (Book 5)
ISBN 979-8-9865173-8-4 (Paperback Edition)

The Warrior and the Archer (Book 6)
ISBN 979-8-9865173-9-1 (Paperback Edition)

Also available in the Dream Travelers Quest series (the prequel)

Into the Book of Light (Book 1)
ISBN 978-0-9968124-6-7 (Paperback Edition)

The Curse of Shadow Man (Book 2)
978-0-9968124-7-4 (Paperback Edition)

The Garden and the Serpent (Book 3)
ISBN 978-0-9968124-8-1 (Paperback Edition)

The Final Judgement (Book 4)
ISBN 978-0-9968124-9-8 (Paperback Edition)

Published by:
Scripturo
PO Box 2618
Keller, Texas 76248

Cover art and design by Manuel Preitano

Printed in the United States of America

Chapter One

ANNELEE DUG HER HEELS into the horse's sides as she entered the Waystation's clearing. Darkness danced on the periphery of her vision. Her breathing felt labored. She didn't dare look down at the marks on her arm, not wanting to waste one single second of the dwindling time she had left. She stopped the horse a few feet from the Waystation and used the remaining ounces of her strength to pull Theo from the horse and drag him into the white, circular building. Once inside, she collapsed beside him onto the cool tile floor.

Lights flickered. The building hummed as if coming to life.

Images flashed through Annelee's mind as her breathing settled and returned to normal. A subtle thrum pulsed in her body as if the building was resuscitating her.

The images came quicker, flooding her mind with

memories of a life she'd forgotten—her mom, dad, and sister, and her friends back home who called her Leah. She imagined herself in her bedroom, texting Theo when she should have been working on a book report. When he didn't answer, she'd decided to play a game on her sister's PlayStation instead.

"Some game," she mumbled to herself as she sat up and examined the familiar blue jeans and sage-green tank top. She ran her fingers through her long blonde hair, remembering how it had been short and black mere seconds ago. She stared at her bare shoulder, the Life Bars now gone.

A gasp echoed behind her, then a groan.

"Theo, are you okay?"

He grunted as he sat up. "I feel like I've been hit by a truck."

Annelee stood and offered him a hand. "Give it a minute. It'll pass."

Theo took her hand and allowed her to pull him to his feet. He paused with his hand in hers.

"Good?" she asked.

He nodded. "I think so." But he didn't release her hand. "Marsuuv had you. I was so worried. I tried to stop him, but I—I ran out of time."

Annelee squeezed his hand. "It's just a game."

"It felt real," Theo murmured. "I thought I'd lost you too."

For a moment, Annelee saw waves of grief play across Theo's face as he once again came to terms with the reality of his parents' deaths. That part wasn't just a game.

"I'm here now," she said. "And I'm not going anywhere." She flashed him a sincere smile. "And for the record, I thought I'd lost you too."

He nodded, examined his arm where the Life Bars used to be, then sighed. "What a crazy game."

"You're telling me." Annelee released his hand and wandered into the center of the Waystation.

"I still don't understand how we're supposed to win this thing if we can't remember," Theo said behind her.

Annelee found the pedestal in the center of the room with the now familiar rule book splayed open across the top.

She skimmed the text and pointed to the page. "Another note from Talya."

"What does it say?" Theo stepped beside her.

"Apparently, we get one more chance to choose an avatar and try to beat the game. This is it—this is the last Waystation, our last chance to win. We'd better strategize and come up with a plan, or else …"

"Or else what?" he asked.

"Or else we'll be stuck in the game. Forever."

"Forever?"

She shrugged. "Talya wasn't clear on that point. But

I think it's safe to assume. Remember," she said under her breath. "We just have to remember."

She watched Theo move to one of the touch screens on the perimeter of the circular room and start swiping through the avatar options. She skimmed a few more pages in the rule book, then joined him at the adjacent console, her mind swirling with an idea. She swiped her finger across the screen, scrolling through her options, until she landed on the archer she'd just played.

"So I have an idea," she said.

"What's that?" Theo asked while tapping the screen.

She faced him. "What if we pick the same avatars as last time?"

Theo tapped the screen again, then turned to stare at her. "Can we do that?"

"I didn't see anything in the rule book saying we couldn't." Annelee tapped the screen to confirm her selection. "See? It's allowing me to choose it again. I mean, think about it. What would happen? Would we remember everything from the last level?" She scrolled to the bottom of the screen. "My backstory is the same. And look, I can even pick the same extra item—the quill and journal."

"Oh," Theo said flatly.

"What?" she asked. "Do you think it's a stupid idea?"

"No," he said, pointing to his screen. "It's just that

I've already selected an avatar."

"Well, go back and choose the warrior then."

Theo tapped the screen. "I can't. My selection is already locked in."

Annelee sidestepped to see his screen. "What did you choose?"

"The savant."

"What's a savant?"

Theo chuckled.

"What's so funny?" she asked, slightly offended.

"A savant is someone who's gifted in a specific field, like music or math." He glanced at her out of the side of his eye. "They're super smart."

"I still don't see why it's so funny."

Theo faced her. "It's funny because between the two of us, you're the smart one with all the clever ways to beat the game." He nudged her. "Maybe you should've been the savant."

Annelee fought back a grin and returned her focus to her own screen. "Well, clearly I'm smart enough without the extra help. Good thing you picked it."

She felt Theo's eyes on her as she finalized her selections.

"So, here's a question for you, Genius," he said. "If I'm the savant and you're the archer, will we know each other? We did the last time because we were both members of William's rebel troop."

"Well, what's your backstory?" she asked.

Theo read the text at the bottom of the screen. "I'm from Viren," he said. "My mother died in childbirth, and my father is an adviser in the King's Guard. It says here he recently became a Dark Rider."

"Interesting," Annelee said, her mind landing on a different thought. "But if I'm the archer, will I remember Theo the warrior? And if so, what will I think happened to him?"

Theo stared at her for a long moment before saying, "This is going to be interesting."

"Yeah. Very."

They held each other's gazes for several long seconds. "So I guess we charge now?" she said.

"I guess so." Theo led the way to the charging room. The seal above the door came to life with a humming glow.

Annelee touched her chest. "I wrote the colors in my journal. But I didn't understand what they meant. I feel like I hardly understand them now."

"You will," Theo said, reaching for her hand. "Once we step inside, we'll remember." The door glided open, and he pulled her through.

"I hope so," Annelee said, feeling a rush of excitement in her veins. "And I need to take better notes in my journal this time."

"Shhh …" Theo hushed her as the door closed behind them.

"I didn't even pay attention to your avatar," she said. "What are you going to look like this time? Is there anything you can tell me that I can write down to jog my memory? And what extra item did you choose?"

Theo reached over and pressed a finger to her lips, then motioned for her to follow him into the center of the room.

A white medallion pulsed with light in the middle of the floor, centered upon a red cross. Bands of white and green divided the otherwise black round walls.

They were standing in the seal.

It was only then that Annelee felt the draw of the charging station's power.

Following Theo's lead, she stepped onto the white medallion and was instantly overwhelmed with the memory of the truth.

Lost in the bliss of the moment, she found herself wondering how she could ever forget again.

The piercing brightness of midday light blinded Theo's eyes as he scanned the clearing. The Waystation was gone. Behind him, Annelee the archer, with short jet-black hair, ripped her satchel from her shoulder and yanked out her journal and quill. She flipped it open.

"Ha! My other notes are still in here!" she said.

He watched her examine her palm as if searching for something, but she quickly abandoned the task and began writing as fast as she could.

He wanted to ask her what she thought of his appearance, but he didn't dare disturb her.

"Theo is Theo," she mumbled under her breath. "Theo is Theo."

He ran a hand over what he knew to be rust-red-colored hair, then smoothed his hands over a plain brown tunic and pants. It was certainly the simplest attire he'd worn as an avatar. He tried to come up with something useful to tell Annelee to write down, but he couldn't focus, not when his mind swirled and bent under a deluge of new information. Words from books he'd read as the savant drifted through his mind: poetry, random facts, and mathematical figures. They unfolded in his brain in an ordered and sprawling layout.

A twig snapped at the edge of the clearing, and Theo wandered away from Annelee to investigate it, led by an uncontrollable curiosity he assumed belonged to his new avatar.

"Remember," Theo coached himself. "Remember

who you are. Remember the seals."

But even as he said it, the words made little sense, as if they were the nonsensical thoughts that occurred before drifting off to sleep.

He glanced over his shoulder to see Annelee scrawling furiously with one hand while gripping her temple with the other. "No, no, no, no, no!" she said to herself. "Remember, remember, remember!"

"Annelee!" he called. "Write something about the book … the Book of … the Book of …" His mind split in two directions. But his body obeyed the insatiable desire to follow the clues.

"Clues?" Theo said aloud.

But inside his mind, he heard his own voice whisper, *Yes, follow the clues.*

He stopped shy of the trees. "Remember," he whispered to himself, not knowing why he said it. He turned to see a young woman behind him, crouched on the ground, staring at an open journal in her hands. But he knew her. Didn't he? Her name was Annelee. Or was it Leah? His thoughts blurred, then a pounding ache slammed into his temples.

"Ah!" Theo gripped the sides of his head and doubled over. After a few agonizing seconds, it passed. And when he looked up again, a girl with short dark hair and the intensity of a warrior stared at him from across the clearing.

She jumped to her feet, dropped her journal, and drew her bow. "Who are you? And what are you doing here?" She scanned the clearing while keeping her weapon trained on him.

"I was about to ask you the same thing," Theo said. He noted the way her eyes darted back and forth frantically. "What are you looking for?" he asked.

She didn't answer and instead cast a quick glance over her shoulder. When she didn't find whatever she was looking for, she returned her stare to him. "Show me your arm," she demanded.

Theo stiffened. "That's an odd request and a little forward of you—"

"I said show me your arm!"

Theo took a step toward her, realizing this girl—whoever she was—knew about his curse. The question was, *how* did she know? "Why don't you show me *your* arm?" he said.

She stared at him for a long moment before saying. "On the count of three, I'll lower my weapon and show you my arm. You'll show me yours at the exact same moment, and if you don't, I'll sink an arrow into your forehead."

Theo blinked. "All right. That sounds … fair."

"One," the girl said, lowering her bow. "Two."

Theo gripped the hem of his sleeve, watching as she did the same.

"Three."

They both lifted their sleeves, each of them revealing five black bars lining the shoulders of their right arms.

"I thought I was the only one," Theo said taking a step toward her.

She shot him a skeptical glance but didn't raise her weapon.

"No," she said. "You're not the only one. There is me. And another." She scanned the clearing once again. "He must not have made it." Her face fell. "I failed him." Tears pooled in her eyes.

"You lost someone to this curse," Theo said, stating it as a fact not as a question.

"I did." She stooped to pick up her bow and returned it to her shoulder, then retrieved the journal she'd dropped.

"So … we can die from it?" he asked.

"Of course we can. That's what these bars represent— our life force." She skimmed her journal then peered up at him. "When were you cursed?"

Theo wandered across the clearing to approach her. She fixed him with a cautious eye but seemed more at ease than when she'd first aimed her bow at him.

"I woke up with the markings yesterday morning after my father refused to join the Dark Riders. He's an adviser in the King's Guard. I can only assume Marsuuv placed this curse upon me as a means to force my father's hand." He glanced down at his booted feet. "Because just this morning my father made his vow to Marsuuv and joined him in a battle against Sir William Atwood and his rebellion." He lifted his eyes to meet hers. "I fled the city in fear, not knowing what else to do. I'm cursed and my father is bound to an evil man …" His voice trailed off. "Surely you must understand."

"More than you know," she said, voice hollow. "I was in the very battle of which you speak."

Theo felt his eyes widen.

"I've even stood face-to-face with Marsuuv. Perhaps more than anyone else, I understand what you're going through."

Theo noted the sadness in her voice. "This person you lost to the curse … It was recent, was it not?" He didn't wait for her to answer. "I'm saddened to hear of your loss." He pressed his lips together, then asked, "What's your name?"

"Annelee." She touched her chest as she said it. "And you?"

"Theodore," he said. "But my father calls me Theo."

A wave of grief washed over her face but was quickly

replaced with a look of rage. She huffed and turned.

"Forgive me," he said. "I've never known someone to be so offended by my name."

He watched her shift from foot to foot, then turn. Redness ringed her eyes. She bit her bottom lip as if to suppress its quiver.

"Theo is the name of my ... my friend I lost."

Theo started to press her about the coincidence, but horse hooves pounded the ground somewhere nearby. Seconds later two Dark Riders burst into the clearing. Behind them a massive silver stallion appeared. A pale-faced man in a black cloak sat upon its back.

Despite the warmth of the sun, a shiver raced down Theo's neck. The marks on his arm burned. And though he didn't understand how he knew it, he whispered the man's name.

"Marsuuv."

Behind him, he heard a bowstring being drawn taut. Annelee stepped up beside him. "On my word, *run*."

The two Dark Riders also drew their bows, but Theo felt no fear, only curiosity.

"Forgive my boldness," he said while pushing Annelee's bow to point at the dirt. "But it's quite small-minded to think the only way out of a situation such as this is through violence."

She jerked her bow back up and scoffed, but Theo

ignored her. Instead, he raised his hands in surrender and stepped forward to meet the mysterious man of shadows who'd cursed him.

"We don't want to fight," Theo called to Marsuuv and his men.

"Speak for yourself," he heard Annelee grumble.

He glanced over his shoulder and motioned for her to follow. She didn't.

"We're not resisting," Theo added, continuing his approach. "We only want to talk."

Marsuuv removed the hood of his cloak revealing a pale, bald scalp lined with thin black veins. "Is that so?" he said in a chilling voice. His thin lips twitched with a smirk. "Then let's talk." His smirk morphed into a sneer. "Guards, seize them."

Chapter Two

THEO SHIFTED, feeling the bark of a tree digging into his back and the abrasive cords of rope cutting into his wrists. Beside him, his new friend, Annelee, was also bound and secured to a tree. When she glanced at him, Theo could tell the fondness he felt for her was not mutual, and she wouldn't be calling him *friend* anytime soon.

He stared through the trees at the edge of clearing, then fixed Marsuuv with his gaze. "I suppose we should have our talk now. Though, I must say, these aren't the conditions I imagined."

Annelee scoffed. "What exactly did you imagine from the monster who cursed us?"

Marsuuv took a step toward them. His Dark Riders stood a pace behind him, one to the left and one to the right.

"What do you want with us?" Annelee demanded.

Marsuuv cocked his pale head and examined them before speaking. "The two of you aren't from this world."

"What?" Annelee said.

Theo's mind grasped at the man's words, seeking to make sense of them.

"Oh, it seems you haven't pieced it together yet." Marsuuv knelt before them. "Interesting that I should know you better than you know yourselves." He stood and, with inhuman speed, drew a dagger from his waist and slit the throats of the two Dark Riders.

Annelee gasped.

The men collapsed with two deafening thuds.

Marsuuv wiped the blade of his knife against his cloak, sheathed it, then knelt in front of Theo and Annelee again. With his spindly fingers he reached for Theo's sleeve, then yanked it up to reveal the five black marks on his shoulder. "As I said, you're not from this world." His icy finger grazed Theo's arm. "So tell me, what world are you from?"

"What does that even mean?" Annelee said. "Of course we're from this world."

Marsuuv looked from her to Theo. "And what say you? After all, it was you who wanted to talk. Or perhaps you'd rather sing me a song." He chuckled as if he'd made a joke. When Theo didn't respond, the man straightened and stood. "So you really don't know where you're from? I suppose that also means you don't know what you're capable of."

Theo's mind whirled, grasping at every word Marsuuv said and matching it up with any relevant information he could find in his memory. The man spoke in riddles, and Theo knew he had to solve them. "What do you mean *what I'm capable of*?" he asked.

"Ah, he does speak. Good. Because your words have great power, Dream Traveler—even your written words. You'll see."

"Dream Traveler," Annelee mumbled, as if the phrase was familiar. "Why did you kill them?" She nodded at the bodies of the two Dark Riders.

Marsuuv interlaced his long fingers in front of him. "I didn't want any witnesses. What we're about to discuss is … sensitive."

"We *are* from this world," Theo said, still stuck on that detail. "After all, you put this curse on us."

"This?" Marsuuv asked, gesturing to the black bars. "That is not my doing. I don't have that particular power." He paused, tilting his head. "Tell me, how is it you don't know where you're from?"

"You still haven't told us what you want with us," Theo said.

"And if this curse isn't from you, who is it from?" Annelee demanded. Theo could tell from the intensity in her voice that she longed to know who was responsible for the death of her friend.

Her friend who shared his name.

His mind lingered on the detail.

"My orders have been clear since the beginning," Marsuuv said, "from my master, Teeleh." He paused dramatically. "End William and Rosaline's betrothal so Teeleh can marry her and seize the Kingdom of Viren. But then you showed up and changed the game." He pursed his thin lips.

"Changed the game," Theo repeated under his breath.

Marsuuv unsheathed his dagger, and with lightning movement, cut the restraints that bound them.

Standing, he cast the ropes aside, then motioned for Theo and Annelee to rise. "You seek something, and I know what it is." He fixed his eyes on Annelee. "You know what it is too."

She shifted.

"But you don't know *where* it is," he added.

"Where is it?" Annelee asked through gritted teeth.

Marsuuv tapped a finger to his chin. "Should I tell you? Hmmm …" He shrugged. "Might as well. The journey to reach it will be treacherous. You'll be lucky if you find it at all."

"The book?" she asked.

"The book?" Theo repeated. An image of a dusty, leather-bound manuscript filled his mind. But when he pictured himself flipping through the yellowed pages, they were all blank.

"Where is it?" Annelee demanded, interrupting his thoughts.

Marsuuv grinned. "In the heart of the Dark Forest."

"Why are you telling us this?" Theo asked, noticing the way Annelee's gaze drifted past Marsuuv and landed on her bow and quiver of arrows leaning against a nearby tree. She shifted on her feet and glanced upward into the boughs of the tree that towered over them.

"No need to pull that clever stunt again, Archer," Marsuuv said.

Theo looked from him to Annelee. Clearly these two had interacted before.

Marsuuv flipped his dagger in his hand and extended the hilt to Annelee. She hesitated, then took it. Marsuuv nodded, satisfied, then took a step backward, clasping his hands at his waist.

"What is this?" Annelee asked, staring at the weapon in her hand.

"Why, a dagger of course."

"I can see that. Why are you giving it to me?"

Marsuuv flashed a now familiar grin.

Theo's stomach turned.

"I thought you wanted to kill me," Marsuuv replied. "Or was that arrow you shot through my gut the last time we met a friendly little way of saying hello?"

Theo snapped his head to look at her.

Annelee narrowed her eyes.

"I know you hate me," Marsuuv said in a taunting tone. "And hatred is the same as murder—or so I once heard someone say. So why not seal the deal?"

"Seal the deal," Theo murmured. "A seal …"

"Come now, dearie. I can see the quiver in your hand. I can feel the pulse of your hatred, warm and sweet like honey—at least, that's how it feels to me. End this. End this now, and you shall win."

The spiderweb of veins on his bald scalp darkened as he spoke.

"Win …" Theo mumbled. "A game …"

"Of course I hate you," Annelee said, jaw clenched. "You've poisoned my king, kidnapped my future queen, and now you're planning to murder all those innocent prisoners you're holding in the dungeon."

"Am I now? And who told you I would do something as heinous as that? As I said," Marsuuv smirked, "the plans have changed."

Annelee stared at him with hate-filled eyes. The dagger trembled in her hand. Her knuckles turned white as she gripped it harder.

"You can't do it, can you?" Marsuuv said. "You *won't* do it. Just as I know you'll never reach the Dark Forest and the book you seek."

"Don't listen to him," Theo said, his voice low. "This isn't how we win." Though, he had no idea what his own words meant.

Annelee ignored him and instead spoke to Marsuuv. "I'm not foolish enough to believe I can kill you with this." She lifted the blade. "I shot you straight through with an arrow and you didn't die."

"Yes," Marsuuv said slowly. "I remember. But this is *my* blade. Perhaps you'll discover it has a different effect."

Theo saw her expression shift.

"Don't." He touched her arm. "It's a trap."

She yanked her arm away.

"Oh, I forgot to tell you how sorry I am," Marsuuv said, his voice dripping with insincerity. "What a shame that your warrior friend didn't make it. At least not in the form you remember..."

Theo felt the energy shift in Annelee's body. Rage pulsed through every cell of her being. He knew her mind was fixed on one thing—killing Marsuuv.

At the same time, Theo's mind was fixed on another.

What did Marsuuv mean by *not in the form you remember*?

"Tell me," Marsuuv said. "Did he suffer?"

Annelee flinched, flicked her wrist, then threw the dagger with expert precision.

The blade stuck in the ground at Marsuuv's feet, pinning his cloak to the earth.

"You're right. I won't do it," she said.

Marsuuv yanked the knife from the ground and sheathed it once again.

"But I *will* reach the Dark Forest," she said through gritted teeth. "And I *will* find the book."

"Oh, will you?" Marsuuv said. He raised his eyebrows. "That I would like to see." With a swoosh of his cloak, he turned. The hem of the fabric billowed behind him as he marched six paces into the forest, then stepped behind a tree.

Shaken from his thoughts, Theo rushed to follow him, but when he reached the tree, Marsuuv was gone.

Chapter Three

THEO SCRATCHED HIS HEAD and once again searched the area behind the tree where Marsuuv had disappeared mere seconds before. Though they were in a forest, he shouldn't have been able to vanish. The brush wasn't thick enough, the trees not dense enough. There was only one explanation.

"He's not human," Theo mumbled.

"Of course he's not," Annelee said, retrieving her bow and quiver. She slung them over her shoulder and sighed. "Look, this was fun. You know, facing off with an evil monster together, but I've got to get out of here. Surely my comrades are wondering where I am, and now I need to plan a mission to the Dark Forest to retrieve some kind of book."

"I'll go with you," Theo said.

"No. You won't. You'll return to wherever you came from and leave me to my business."

"It's my business too."

She adjusted her satchel, then shot him a look. "How do you figure?"

Theo allowed himself to sink deeper into his own mind, pulling forward an image of a dusty old book. He could almost smell the aged paper that filled it. Blank pages. One of them dotted with reddish-brown stains. "I'm also in search of a book," he said. "And I feel certain it's the same one you seek."

"What makes you so certain?"

Theo lifted his sleeve, glanced down at the five bars that marked his arm, then said, "We're not from this world."

Annelee sighed. "Don't let Marsuuv work his way into your mind. He's a devil and a trickster."

"Then clearly this is a trap."

"What is?"

"Him sending us into the heart of the Dark Forest."

"No, not *us*," Annelee said. "*Me*."

Theo replayed Marsuuv's words. "Tell me about this warrior friend of yours, the one you lost to the curse."

Annelee's face darkened. "I will not speak of such private matters with a stranger."

"Perhaps I'm not a stranger," Theo pressed.

She cut him with her glare. "Stop with your riddles and speak plainly."

"Very well. Do you understand what Marsuuv meant when he said it was a shame your warrior friend didn't make it? 'At least not in the form you remember.'"

She scowled.

"What? You said to speak plainly." He watched the waves of emotion play across her face, feeling each one as if they were his own. "You cared deeply for this friend. Perhaps … perhaps he was even more than a friend."

Annelee sniffed and turned to look away.

"Please don't hate me for saying this."

"For saying what?" she asked, still not looking at him.

Theo chewed the inside of his lip before speaking. "Perhaps I am Theo."

She snapped her head in his direction. "You already said that's your name."

"Yes, but …" He stepped closer, until he was no more than an arm's length away from her. She smelled like fresh air, sunshine, and strawberries. "Perhaps I am *your* Theo."

She stared at him for a long moment. Her lips parted as if to protest, but she didn't speak, didn't look away. After several seconds, the intensity on her face softened. "Impossible."

"It would be," he said. "If we were from this world."

She nodded slowly. "But we're not."

"Precisely."

"Then what does that mean?"

"It means your ties to William and your team of rebels are no longer relevant. The only thing that matters is this book."

"How do you know this? How do you know the book is significant but not William?"

"That I don't know, but I'm certain the book is significant. Ever since I was a small child, my mind has worked in unusual ways. When I think of this book it feels …" He paused to search for the words. "It feels real to me. Almost as if I have a memory of it." He held her stare. "It's the same way I feel about you. You feel real to me."

She looked away. "Theo is Theo," she said under her breath.

"What was that?"

She swung her satchel around to the front and began searching its contents. Seconds later she pulled out a leather-bound journal. She flipped it open.

"Theo is Theo." She tapped the page with her index finger. "What if you're right? What if you are my … what if you are the Theo I once knew." She flipped back a couple pages. "Look at these notes here. This one is about Shataiki and human blood."

As she said it, an image of a black winged batlike beast flashed through Theo's mind.

"I made this note long before I understood what it meant. And this one I still haven't figured out."

Theo glanced down at the page and read aloud. "White, green, black, red, and white."

Again, images filled his mind.

A sword with gemstones inlaid on the hilt.

A glowing medallion crest.

Five doors of the same four colors.

Without understanding why, he reached his left hand to his right shoulder.

"Theo is Theo," Annelee repeated. "I think you're right."

"Which would mean your mission is my mission, and I must accompany you to the Dark Forest and help you find this book."

"There's a problem with that plan," she said. "The Dark Forest is crawling with Shataiki. My fellow rebels narrowly escaped with their lives when they entered. We'll surely be killed, even with this knowledge of using human blood as poison. There are far too many of them. I think you're right. It must be a trap."

"But you're quite skilled with your bow, are you not?"

"I am."

"Then trap or no trap, it's a risk we must take. What

other choice do we have? We must retrieve this book."

Her eyes drifted past him, but she nodded. "And if we know it's a trap, we can be alert."

"Precisely," Theo said. "Now, Marsuuv mentioned Teeleh. What do you know of him?"

"Not much. Only that he's Marsuuv's master and is bound to the territory of the Dark Forest. My commanding officer, William, mentioned it when he was trying to convince us to go into the forest to rescue Rosaline." She straightened. "Rosaline! She's in the Dark Forest. Or at least, William was convinced we'd find here there."

"Rescue the princess," Theo said. "Save the Kingdom of Viren, and find a book."

Annelee tilted her head as if he'd just said the most profound words she'd ever heard. "Yes. Yes, you're right. We must find both Rosaline and the book."

"And in doing so, we save Viren."

Annelee closed her journal and tucked it back into her satchel.

Theo wandered away.

"Where are you going?"

"The Dark Riders' horses are over here. We're going to need them."

She jogged to catch up with him. "Theo," she said hesitantly, then added, "It feels strange to call you that."

He glanced over his shoulder. "It may feel strange for you to speak it, but nothing else has ever felt so right as for me to hear you say it."

Her face flushed. "I was just thinking: if we're not from this world, then what world are we from?"

Images flashed through his mind once more, swirling and mingling with no sense or rhythm. "From another earth I suppose. In time, I shall solve this mystery. But now, it matters not where we are from, only where we're going."

Theo quickened his pace, realizing the location of their destination was as much a mystery as their origin. The only thing he knew was its name—the Dark Forest.

William sat silently beside the campfire, lost in thought and mesmerized by flames. Around him, his men slept. Only Conrad remained awake, eyes trained on him from across the fire.

"You don't need to babysit me, Conrad. I am the prince of Viren."

"The soon-to-be prince," Conrad said, voice flat. "I'm worried about you. You had great losses in the battle today. The loss of your alliance with Saxum and the loss of many great men and women, including

Wolf and Hawk." He paused. "I know those two were important to you."

Without looking up from the fire, William said, "Let's not forget the innocent prisoners who will be executed. And Rosaline."

"I could never forget them. Or her. Just as you never will."

"You make it sound as though I shall never find her."

"I didn't say that—"

"I will find her," William said.

"*We* will find her," Conrad corrected.

William stood. "Thank you for sitting up with me. And thank you for your loyalty." He came around the fire to stand before Conrad and extended his right arm to him. They clasped each other's forearms. "I believe I should like to retire to my sleeping mat now. Must you also watch me while I sleep, or can a soon-to-be prince have his dignity and privacy?"

Conrad dipped his head. "As you wish, my lord. But I shall be close."

"As you always are."

William wandered away from the fire and found his bed for the night. He heard Conrad settle a few yards away.

Flat on his back, William stared up at the starless sky. Only the moon provided a faint glow, hidden behind wispy thin clouds.

He sighed, his soul feeling as dark as the night. He'd done his best to hide his despair from Conrad, but his second-in-command knew him all too well. And he'd never allow William to do what was necessary.

He had to get to the Dark Forest to rescue Rosaline.

Eventually, the gentle snores of Conrad reached William's ears. He rolled to his side and stared off into the night, his mind racing through options of what to do next.

William's gaze landed on a dark shape between two trees. In the thick of night, he thought his eyes might be playing tricks on him, but then the figure moved.

It was human.

William quietly sat up and glanced around at his camp. All rebels were accounted for—at least, those who'd made it through the battle.

Reaching for his nearby sword, William stood and wandered toward the visitor.

He approached silently, watching for the figure to move again. Either he'd been mistaken, or this person was waiting for him. When he reached the two trees, the clouds parted just enough for the faint streams of moonlight to illuminate the figure's face.

"Marsuuv," William whispered.

"Hello, William."

"Where is Rosaline? Tell me now!"

"Keep your voice low," Marsuuv said in a chilling whisper.

"Why?" William demanded, touching the hilt of his sword. "Are you not here to kill me?"

"Me? Kill you?" Marsuuv let out a low chuckle.

"I don't see what's so funny. You've only been hunting me for weeks now." William's fingers wrapped around his weapon.

Marsuuv held up a hand to still William's actions. "Funny story," Marsuuv said with a smirk. "I can't kill you. Nor do I need to."

William narrowed his eyes.

"I know, I know. Absurd, isn't it? But it's true. My power has its limits."

"I don't understand," William said, hand resting on his weapon. "You drew a target on my back. I've been in hiding, running for my life, and—"

"Yes, but you're no longer the target of my interests," Marsuuv interrupted. "Someone else is. Someone not from this world."

William's mind whirled, trying to make sense of Marsuuv's words. "And what of Rosaline?" he demanded. "Where is she?"

Marsuuv's lips twitched. "Oh, I thought you knew where we've been keeping her."

William's eyes darted back and forth, searching the

night. "The Dark Forest—I was right. She's with your master, Teeleh. Who is he, and what does he want with her?"

"The same thing you want with her," Marsuuv said with a devious grin. "To wed her and seize the Kingdom of Viren. Like you, he's using her as a mere pawn in his plan to obtain power."

"That's not what I am doing! I love her!"

"Oh, come now, Prince. It's just us. You can tell me the truth. I mean, do you even find her beautiful?"

"She's the love of my life! Don't you dare speak of her this way!"

"The love of your life?" Marsuuv feigned surprise. "I never would have guessed. I mean, with all your running about to save King Tyrus and create alliances with the queen of Saxum, it seems clear to me that Rosaline is an afterthought in your great plan."

"How dare you! I should have killed you when I had the chance. I never should have listened to Conrad and the others. I should have followed my instincts." William drew his sword.

"Ah, ah, ah. I wouldn't do that if I were you."

"And why not?" William poised, ready to strike. "You can't do anything about it. You just said you can't kill me."

"True," Marsuuv said. "I can't. But they can." He

lifted his hand in a signal, and six Dark Riders emerged from the forest, swords drawn.

William took a step back.

Marsuuv sneered, lowered his hand, and said, "Do as you like with him, then take him to our master."

William braced, sword poised, prepared to fight for his life, when an arrow sailed past his ear and sank into the forehead of the nearest Dark Rider. He spun, hearing the sound of booted feet running through the forest. Three silhouettes appeared against the fading fire of the rebel camp; William would recognize them anywhere: Conrad, Elijah, and Liam.

He ducked when he saw Elijah nock another arrow.

Shouts echoed through the trees, and within seconds the entire rebel camp was awake and rushing to save their prince.

William spun, hearing one of Marsuuv's men let out a cry of pain. The Dark Rider grasped at his shoulder where Elijah's arrow now protruded. Another dart flew through the night, then sank into the man's chest.

William sensed movement to his left. He swung his sword to block a blow from one of the other Dark Riders. A clash rang out as metal collided with metal. He gritted his teeth, arms quivering as he held back his opponent. The Dark Rider leaned into his sword with all his weight. William's body trembled.

Seconds later, Conrad appeared at William's side through the darkness and plunged his sword into the gut of the Dark Rider. The man sank to the ground with a groan.

"Get back!" Conrad commanded William.

"I will not back down and leave my men—"

"I said get back!" Conrad shouted. "If you die, Viren will be lost!"

Out of the corner of his eye, William saw Marsuuv slink back into the shadows, leaving his three remaining Dark Riders to finish what he couldn't. Marsuuv's teeth gleamed with a sinister smile, then he was gone.

Conrad shoved his hand against William's chest as Liam rushed past them, weapon drawn. "Get back," Conrad said. "Get back and let us do our job!"

The sounds of battle rang out all around him, but William knew what he had to do. He also knew he'd never forgive himself for this moment. He took off running back toward their camp, regretting his actions with every step. He'd never left his fellow warriors' sides. But as Conrad had said, if William died, all would be lost—including Rosaline.

And now that William knew for certain where he could find her, he would never allow that to happen.

William sprinted through the forest, hearing the sounds of his loyal rebels fighting on his behalf.

Through the darkness, he spotted his horse. He sheathed his sword as he reached it, untied the animal, and swung himself up and onto its back. Snapping the reins, he dug his heels into the horse's sides. It let out a loud snort, then took off at a gallop.

"William!" Conrad shouted. "William! Where are you going?"

William clenched his teeth and hunched over the horse's neck, knowing he had to distance himself from his men as quickly as possible if he was to outrun them. He couldn't risk them following him, though he knew they'd try anyway.

As their leader, he'd never lead them into such danger.

But as Rosaline's betrothed, he had no other choice.

Marsuuv was wrong.

William loved Rosaline. And everything he'd done over the past few weeks, he'd done for her.

Including this.

"William!" He heard Conrad shout again. "Where are you going?"

William gripped tighter to the reins and pushed the horse to run faster. Under his breath, he said, "I'm going to the Dark Forest."

Chapter Four

THE MIDMORNING SUN glimmered off the vibrant waters of the Emerald River. Theo stared at the Dark Forest on the opposite side. It had taken them a day and a half to reach Viren's eastern border, plus one night of making camp for a few hours of rest for themselves and their horses.

"I've heard stories of this river," Annelee said. "But I never imagined it would look so vibrant."

"Green," Theo said under his breath, his mind returning to the list of colors from Annelee's journal. He urged his horse toward a rickety bridge, but the animal resisted and stomped its hooves.

"C'mon," Theo said, nudging it again.

"What's wrong?" Annelee said.

"I don't know. He's skittish about something."

"The Dark Forest, probably."

Theo glanced across the river at the bright-green foliage that lined the other side. "I don't understand what's so dark about it. The forest looks nearly identical to the one on this side."

"Looks can be deceiving," Annelee said. "One of my comrades, Liam, told me the story of the rebels' encounters with this forest during our travels to Saxum. Trust me. It's darker in there than you can imagine."

Theo swallowed. "But we have no other choice." Once again, he urged the horse to move toward the bridge. It obeyed reluctantly, tossing its mane and giving a protesting snort.

They stopped at the bridgehead. Moss covered the broken boards, reflecting the deep-green color of the narrow river that flowed beneath it. A feeling like déjà vu washed over Theo. He noted it, then took the lead across the bridge. The boards groaned beneath them.

"I don't think this is going to hold," Annelee called from behind him. "Not with the weight of the horses."

Theo ignored her and pushed across the bridge as quickly as possible. He exhaled when they finally touched the bank on the other side, not realizing he'd been holding his breath. The stench of mildew greeted him.

"Look!" Annelee drew up beside him and pointed straight ahead. "Liam was right."

The once vibrant-green and alive forest now towered in front of them with dark, dying foliage. Gnarled, bare branches twisted toward the sky, supported by massive black tree trunks.

"C'mon," she said, leading her horse through the thick layers of decomposing leaves. "We don't want to linger."

Theo nudged his resistant horse and followed Annelee, who led them onto a barely distinguishable path through the trees.

"Keep a look out for white lilies," she called back to him.

"White?" Theo asked, his mind continuing to work on the mysterious list of colors.

"Yeah. The air of this forest is filled with a toxin. We'll need the lilies if we're going to survive." She glanced back at him. "Let's hope they work. William said they helped him and his men when they entered the forest, but they weren't as effective for King Tyrus."

Theo nodded, feeling a heaviness in his head as he did. His thoughts clouded. He forced himself to stay focused.

"White," he mumbled to himself. "White lilies. Green—a green river. Black—the Dark Forest."

"What are you saying back there?"

"Nothing," Theo called ahead. "Just thinking aloud."

"Well, don't get too lost in your thoughts. This is a dangerous place. Stay alert."

"I will," Theo said. But he felt his hazy mind wander to a soft song that drifted on the breeze.

"Do you hear that?" he asked.

Annelee turned in the saddle. "Hear what?"

"It sounds like … humming. Like a song. It's familiar."

She pressed her lips together and listened, then shook her head. "I don't hear anything. It must be the toxin messing with your mind. C'mon. We need to find the white lilies before it's too late."

Theo picked up the pace, following her deeper into the Dark Forest while trying to ignore the clear, crystal tone that resonated in his ears.

A flash of white caught his eye to the left. "I think I saw something."

Annelee wavered in her saddle.

"Annelee?" he called.

When she turned to look at him, her face was pale.

He pulled his horse alongside hers.

"I don't feel so good," she mumbled.

Theo caught her arm as she started to slump forward.

"I think we're close. Hold on." He reached across her to grab the reins of her horse and jerked the animal to a stop. Then, after swinging his leg over the side of his own horse, he took off in a sprint toward the white he'd seen through the trees.

Several yards into the dense brush, he stumbled, overcome by a woozy feeling. "No, no, no. I can do this." He collected himself, then took off again, trying desperately to continue in a straight line. He saw another splash of white amid the dark foliage.

"White," he mumbled, feeling delirious. "White. The light is infinite." His words made no sense. His vision blurred as he reached the stark patch of flowers. Dropping to his knees, he plucked a bloom and instinctively shoved the entire thing into his mouth and began chewing. Within seconds, his head cleared. He quickly picked all the blooms he could find in the small area and rushed back to Annelee. When he found her, she was on the ground, doubled over and heaving.

"Here, eat this." He shoved a flower into her hand.

Color returned to her cheeks as she chewed.

"Thank you," she said, flopping into a seated position.

Theo collapsed beside her. "I have more."

She waved him away. "I'm feeling better. Besides, we should hold onto the extra lilies in case we need them later."

"Good idea." He stood and tucked them into his saddlebag. When he finished, he turned to find Annelee staring at him.

"What?" he asked.

She shook her head. "I'm just trying to imagine you as Theo—my Theo. It still doesn't make sense."

Theo tightened the straps of the saddlebag. "Often the logical mind can't see the truth of reality."

She rolled her eyes and grinned. "My Theo would never say something as absurd as that."

He returned the smile and offered her a hand, pulling her to her feet. "Well your Theo sounds quite dull."

"He wasn't dull. He was the bravest warrior I ever knew. He even defeated a giant to save me and my comrades. He was brave and kind."

He stared into her deep-green eyes, overcome with a sense of familiarity. "How do you know I'm not brave and kind?"

"I don't know anything about you." She smirked. "But I suppose I'll learn. After all, we are stuck with each other for now." She gestured to the towering trees of the Dark Forest.

Theo ignored the jab, unable to look away from her. "I don't know what it is, but I feel connected to you." He reached out, hesitated, then touched the choppy ends of her short black hair. She didn't push him away.

"I hate to admit it, but I do too."

"Because Theo is Theo?" he said, playfully raising

his eyebrows.

"Ah, you made a joke." This time she did push his hand away. "Brave, kind, and funny? Perhaps you are an upgraded Theo."

He shifted to a more serious tone. "Or perhaps it's because we're not from this world."

She sighed. "But what does that even mean? I've been thinking about it nonstop during our travels. I *know* I'm from this world. I have family from this world. I have memories from this world."

The word *memories* struck him. "Maybe that's just part of the game."

"A game? Why would you say that?"

"I don't know. It's just an idea that keeps coming to me."

"But it isn't a game, Theo. It's life."

He shrugged. "But isn't life just a game? And we're all characters playing our roles, avatars, so to speak?"

She rolled her eyes again. "Now that sounds like something I've heard before, from someone older and *much* wiser." Her eyes drifted past him with a faraway look. An expression of confusion quickly replaced it, but before Theo could ask her about it, a screech echoed overhead.

They both snapped their attention upward.

"Shataiki," Theo said quietly.

"How do you know?"

"I don't know. I just do."

She pulled an arrow from her quiver, removed her bow from her shoulder, then paused, listening. "I wonder why we haven't seen any of the beasts yet," she said in a whisper.

The boughs of a nearby tree bounced. Leaves rustled.

Annelee held the tip of her arrow against her palm, ready to drag it across her flesh and coat it with a layer of human blood, when Theo stopped her.

"Wait, look." He pointed toward the tree. A flash of white appeared through the dense leaves. "I don't think it's a—"

A giant white batlike creature burst through the foliage and landed at their feet.

In the span of seconds, Annelee cut her palm, coated the dart, and nocked the arrow. She took aim, muscles quivering in her strong arms as she held back the bowstring. "It is a Shataiki!" she shouted.

"Who, me?" the creature asked while peering back at her with wide green eyes. "Oh, no, no, no. I'm not a Shataiki. I'm a Roush. Sebastian, remember?"

Theo tilted his head and stared at the creature. There was something familiar about it, though he was certain he'd never seen it before.

"Ah, yes. That's right. You're *new* to this game."

"A game," Theo repeated.

Annelee looked between Theo and Sebastian. "Should I shoot it?"

Sebastian made a disgusted face. "I'd prefer you didn't."

Theo smirked, then placed a hand on Annelee's shoulder. "I think he's a friend not a foe."

"Oh yes, yes, yes. I'm a friend. And a very good friend, indeed."

Annelee lowered her weapon.

"You said you're a Roush?" The word felt familiar on Theo's tongue. "What are you doing here in the Dark Forest?"

"I live here, of course."

"Alone with the Shataiki?"

Sebastian waddled a step closer. "Not alone. I'm never alone. And yes, the Shataiki are here, but I pay them no mind, and they don't bother me. In fact, I barely notice their presence."

Theo felt his shoulders drop and his body relax. "So they can't hurt us?"

"Oh yes, yes, yes, they can surely hurt you."

Theo stiffened again.

"But only because you've forgotten who you are." Sebastian extended his batlike wings to the sides, then folded them once again.

"No, we've figured out that much," Annelee said, returning her bow to her shoulder and blotting her bloodied palm on her pants. "Theo is Theo." She examined her hand.

"Ah, yes, yes, yes. Theo is Theo. But do you know who Theo is?" Sebastian blinked.

Annelee glanced up from her palm. "Huh?"

"Mmm …" Sebastian nodded. "Not to worry, my friends. Soon you'll understand. And then you'll win."

"Win?" Theo repeated. He exchanged a glance with Annelee. She shrugged.

"Yes. Win. Now come, come, come. We have much ground to cover and little time to do so." He started to waddle forward. "Oh." He turned. "Speaking of time … How much time do you have left?"

Theo and Annelee stared at him.

The Roush motioned for them to lift their sleeves.

Finally understanding, both Theo and Annelee exposed their shoulders and the four remaining bars that marked their arms.

"Well?" Annelee asked. "You seem to know more than we do. How much time do we have left?"

Sebastian waddled closer to examine the tattoolike marks. "Hmmm … Enough," he said with a nod, then shrugged. "I think."

Annelee hesitated, then tugged her sleeve back down.

"As I'm sure you've figured out by now, time is not the only factor that's of the essence. You'd be wise to conserve your energies as well." He eyed Annelee's bow.

She shifted it on her shoulder. "Understood."

"Good. Now as I was saying, come, come, come."

"Where are you taking us?" Theo asked while swinging his leg over his horse.

"To the heart of the Dark Forest, of course."

"You know of it?" Theo asked. "I mean, surely you do. You live here."

"I know it not because I live here but because it's in my programming."

Theo furrowed his brow and directed his horse to follow Sebastian, who was now gliding through the air in front of them.

"So where is it?" Theo asked.

Sebastian executed a barrel roll, then continued forward. "It is not a *where* but a *what*." He hummed a tune as he flapped his wings.

"Then *what* is it?" Annelee asked, riding up alongside Theo.

In front of them, the trail widened.

"Teeleh's castle, of course. Now, come, come, come."

Sebastian continued humming as he led them

through the path of snaking black vines and dark, towering trees. Theo couldn't help but notice it was the same tune he'd heard when they'd first entered the Dark Forest. After a few notes, he found himself humming along. The song welled up inside him, and yet, he couldn't place it. As if he'd known it since childhood but had forgotten.

"Life is a cycle of remembering and forgetting," Theo whispered.

"Talking to yourself again?" Annelee asked.

Theo chuckled but said nothing, unable to shake the sound of an equally familiar and unsettling voice echoing in his mind, saying, *Remember.*

Chapter Five

THEY MADE CAMP AT DUSK, at Sebastian's insistence. Theo unpacked the saddlebag, happy to see that the Dark Riders, whose horses they'd taken, had been well prepared for long-distance travel. He spread out a sleeping pad, watching Annelee set hers up on the opposite side of the fire they'd built. Theo settled onto the mat, weary from travel, and scanned their surroundings.

During their journey, the scenery of the Dark Forest had shifted from decay to lush foliage—all of it black: the plush grass beneath Theo's mat, the giant tropical leaves that surrounded their camp, even the wood they'd found for the fire—all of it as dark as a midnight sky. The only splashes of color in the otherwise blackened world came from the various pieces of fruit dangling from the darkened vines.

"There's a lot of fruit in this part of the forest," Theo

said, sitting up. "Is it edible? Our rations are getting low."

Sebastian waddled up beside him and joined Theo on his mat. Across from them, Annelee removed her boots and stretched out on her back.

"Yes, there are many fruits in this area," the Roush said. "However, the fruit in this forest isn't merely for sustenance."

"What do you mean?" Annelee asked, rolling onto her side to look at him.

"The fruits here have abilities: some keep you from dreaming, some heal, others give you great power." He paused. "But others are quite deadly. Since you're not familiar with them, it would be best to avoid them. Even I, though I live here, am not well versed in all the many fruits and their powers. It's not in my programming."

Theo noted Sebastian's use of the word *programming* again.

The sun drifted lower in the sky and filtered through the black trees with a haunting glow. Both Theo and Annelee reclined on their mats, chewing on pieces of jerky. For a moment, Theo occupied himself with thoughts of Annelee, wondering if she might be thinking of him as well. But his attention quickly shifted to the puzzle at hand: what did Marsuuv mean when he'd said they were not from this world?

The clues swirled in his mind.

Soon you'll understand, and then you'll win, Sebastian had said.

A game ...

Programming ...

"White, green, black, red, and white," Theo whispered to himself. The list of colors gnawed at his mind, as if they'd long ago held meaning but somehow he'd forgotten.

Life is a cycle of remembering and forgetting.

Remember ...

Theo is Theo.

He grasped his temples and squeezed his eyes closed, trying to fit the pieces together. When he opened them, three pairs of beady red eyes stared down at him from the tree canopy. He bolted upright.

"There's something up there!" he said in a loud whisper while pointing.

As he said it, three giant black bats landed on a nearby tree.

Annelee snatched up her bow. "Shataiki?" she asked, looking at Sebastian.

"Yes," Theo breathed, still not sure how he knew.

"They're not advancing," Annelee said, still gripping her bow, prepared to take down the beasts.

"They look just as I'd imagined," Theo said louder than he intended.

"Of course they do," Sebastian answered.

One of the creatures dropped from the tree and landed no more than ten feet from Theo. It stared deep into his eyes, then spread its wings, hunched its shoulders, and hissed.

An overwhelming urge to sing rose within Theo. He swallowed, realizing how absurd the idea sounded. Instead, he watched the Shataiki fold its wings, then slowly back away. They hunkered down in the trees.

"Why are they not attacking?" Annelee asked while lowering her weapon.

"They've been instructed not to," Sebastian said, as if the fact should have been clear.

Annelee snapped her attention to Sebastian. "By whom?"

The Roush blinked his big green eyes. "By Teeleh. Who else?"

Annelee exchanged a glance with Theo.

"The master of the Dark Forest wants to see you," Sebastian clarified. "Preferably alive. And so he will!" he added with a little too much enthusiasm.

A chill worked its way through Theo's shoulders. He stared past Annelee at a strange leafy black plant. A dozen or more lemon-shaped pieces of fruit dangled from its vines, rich with the colors of the sunset. Beyond the trees, Theo noticed for the first time a mountain in the near distance.

"Sebastian. What mountain is that?"

The Roush followed his gaze. "That? Oh, that is Mount Mori—the Mountain of Death."

Theo turned to look at him.

"Where Teeleh lives, of course."

"We're going up there?" Annelee asked.

"Indeed!" Sebastian said. "Now, best to get some rest. It's a grueling climb. We'll begin our ascent at first light." He made himself comfortable at the end of Theo's mat, curling up like a pup at his feet. "Sweet dreams!" he said, then closed his bright-green eyes.

"Dreams," Theo murmured.

He stretched out once more and rolled onto his side, unsure if he could even doze under the watchful red eyes of the Shataiki.

"Annelee?"

"Hmmm?" She scanned their camp before reclining. She made herself comfortable but kept her bow tucked beneath her arm.

"Does the phrase *Dream Traveler* mean anything to you? Marsuuv said it."

Her lips twitched as her eyes held his from across the fire. "It sounded familiar when he said it ..." Her voice drifted. "But I don't know why. And no, I don't know what it means."

"Me either," Theo said, recalling Marsuuv had also mentioned that Theo's words held great power. Whatever that meant.

"I'm starting to believe him," Theo finally said.

"Believe who?"

"Marsuuv." Theo tucked his arm under his cheek. "I don't think we're from this world."

Annelee stared at him for a long moment before saying, "I think you're right." She flipped over onto her other side. "Good night," she called over her shoulder.

Theo stared at her back, knowing that with her warrior instincts, she probably wouldn't sleep.

And with the unsolved mysteries that swarmed in his mind, neither would he. Despite Sebastian's insistence, there would be no dreaming for either of them that night.

Theo stood at the top of the mountain, staring up at a sprawling gothic-style castle, complete with ornate spires and Shataiki gargoyles. Annelee stopped her horse beside Theo's and dismounted, then took the reins of both and found a nearby tree where she could tie them up. Sebastian, who'd been riding on top of Theo's horse's head, dropped to the ground and followed Annelee back to Theo.

"There's something familiar about this place," Annelee said as she joined him.

"The castle?" Sebastian asked.

"No, the mountain …" The howling of an ominous wind that whipped through the castle's many towers drowned out her voice.

Theo nodded but said nothing. He'd been thinking the same thing during their journey up the steep terrain.

They'd left their camp early that morning under the watchful eyes of hundreds of roosting Shataiki. The beastly creatures had even followed them up the winding hillside. Though they'd hissed and occasionally shrieked, the batlike creatures had kept their distance, acting more as herding animals to ensure Theo and Annelee reached their destination. Thankfully, Theo had managed to ignore their threatening stares, his mind instead occupied by the strange thought that he'd find a cavern near the top of the mountain. A cave with five doors inside: one white, one green, one black, one red, and lastly another white.

Despite Sebastian having informed them of the peak's name—Mount Mori—Theo found himself wanting to call it Mount Veritas.

And like all the other strange thoughts that swirled in his mind, he had no idea as to why.

"Veritas," he said.

Annelee looked at him.

"It means 'truth' in the old language," he added. "That's what we need to do. We need to discover the truth."

Annelee turned back toward the ominous yet beautiful castle and shivered. "Well, let's hope the truth is easy to find. This place gives me the creeps." She pointed at one of the Shataiki gargoyles.

"Yes, yes, yes," Sebastian said. "For your sake, I also hope you find it quickly." He turned and began waddling away. "Best of luck to you both."

"You're not coming with us?" Annelee said.

"Oh no, no, no. You must continue without me. My programming only allows me to go this far."

"What's this programming you keep mentioning?" Theo asked, but when he turned, Sebastian had already taken to the sky.

"Good-bye for now!" the Roush called as he ascended. "And remember!"

"Remember what?" Annelee asked.

"Precisely!" Sebastian shouted, then swooped over the side of the mountain and out of view.

Theo and Annelee held each other's stares. She drew

her bow from her shoulder and prepared an arrow.

Theo motioned toward the towering wooden door at the front of the castle. "Ladies first," he said.

Annelee shot him a curious look, then moved swiftly up the giant stone slab steps that led to the castle's entrance.

"The door is open," she said when Theo reached the top. She pulled the bowstring taut, nudged the door open the rest of the way with her shoulder, then entered arrow first. Theo stepped in beside her.

A gust of refreshingly cool air greeted them along with the welcoming sound of orchestral music.

Ahead of Theo, Annelee lowered her bow. "Whoa. Look at this place." Her voice echoed through the opulent foyer.

Theo took in the scene. Mahogany floors stretched in front of them, warmed by the light of an ornate chandelier. The candles in the fixture flickered invitingly, their firelight glinting off the various pieces of gold décor throughout the room.

"Look at this!" Annelee rushed into the sitting room to the right of the foyer and paused in front of an odd piece of furniture with a giant trumpetlike feature. "The music is coming from here!"

He started to follow her but found himself distracted by one of his other senses. When he drew in a deep breath through his nostrils, his mouth watered and his stomach rumbled.

"Do you smell that?" Theo followed the scent toward a door down the hallway, passing a red velvet chaise longue stacked with pillows and a single leather-bound book. He paused, his fingers grazing the cover. Annelee appeared beside him.

"The book?"

Theo shook his head. "No. That would be too easy."

"Something smells delicious."

He heard her stomach growl.

"It's coming from in there." He pointed to the door.

"Your turn to go first," she said.

He nodded. "Yes, but you're the one with the weapon."

"I thought you were going to prove your bravery?" she said playfully, then pointed an arrow at the door and gestured for Theo to open it for her.

The warm scent of bread wafted through as he swung it open. He stepped in behind Annelee. They both froze. A giant wooden table stretched in front of them, spanning the length of the dining room. Various breads, roasted meats, and assorted side dishes lined the candlelit table, taunting Theo and Annelee with their delicious scents. Even the broccoli smelled good.

Another one of the strange music machines sat in the corner, filling the dining hall with a familiar tune.

Theo tried to place it but was distracted when a door in the back wall swung open. A women entered, facing backward, dressed in an ornate rose-red ballgown. When she turned, Theo saw the silver platter she carried, stacked high with assorted pastries.

Annelee grabbed Theo's forearm and stifled a gasp.

"Oh! You're here," the woman said. "And earlier than expected." She set the platter on the table. "I haven't quite finished the preparations. Give me one moment." She disappeared back through the door into what Theo assumed to be the kitchen. She returned a moment later, humming along to the tune while carrying a pitcher of water.

"Come, have a seat!" Excitement filled her voice. She motioned toward the red velvet-cushioned chairs that lined the table.

Theo took note of the wide smile that lingered on her full cherry-colored lips. The bright color contrasted with her porcelain complexion. Raven-black hair tumbled around her shoulders in soft waves.

She was stunning, more striking even in person, Theo thought. And yet, she looked undeniably like every image he'd ever seen of her.

There was no mistaking her, not even here in Teeleh's castle.

It was Rosaline.

Chapter Six

THEO WATCHED ROSALINE tuck a strand of hair behind her ear, then place the pitcher on the table. She made her way to the head seat and again motioned for Theo and Annelee to sit.

"Come now," she said, adjusting the billowy layers of her dress as she pulled out her chair and took her place at the table. "You must be weary from your travels. And hungry, I hope. I've been cooking all morning. Please don't make me eat lunch by myself." She flashed a playful grin. "Welcome to my castle! My name is Rosaline."

"Yes, Your Highness," Annelee said as she cautiously stepped toward the table. "We know who you are. My friend and I are from Viren."

Theo noticed she'd finally called him her *friend*.

"Oh, from Viren. How lovely. Yes, my darling didn't say where you're from. But of course that matters not to me."

"Your darling? Do you mean William?" Annelee asked, perking up. "Is he here?"

Rosaline didn't seem to hear the question. "The food is getting cold. Won't you please sit?"

Annelee pulled out her chair, and Theo took his seat beside her. The scent of the meal overwhelmed him. His stomach gurgled with hunger.

"Don't be bashful," Rosaline urged. "Fill your plates."

Theo discreetly elbowed Annelee. "Is it okay?" he whispered.

"It's Princess Rosaline," Annelee said. "She wouldn't poison us."

Theo watched the princess fill her plate with a scoop of steamed broccoli florets, then reach for a platter of roasted salmon. She caught Theo's eye. "Fish?"

He shook his head, again feeling overcome with a strange sensation that this moment—or a similar one—had happened once before.

Out of the corner of his eye, he saw Annelee begin to dive into the food she'd stacked onto her plate.

"Princess Rosaline?" she said through a mouthful. "You said this is *your* castle. I'm confused. We thought it belonged to someone else."

Theo listened to their conversation while filling his plate with several of the pastries, a generous helping of roasted carrots, and a leg of roast lamb.

"Oh, well it'll be my castle soon enough," Rosaline said with a sweet chuckle. "As soon as I'm wed to Teeleh, of course."

Annelee stiffened beside Theo.

"But in the meantime, he said to make myself at home," Rosaline continued. "He even started growing my favorite flowers in the garden. Oh, and he has some cut every morning to fill the house. Isn't that lovely?"

Theo glanced past the feast to see a bouquet of red roses on a side table. Their color matched Rosaline's dress.

Annelee dabbed her lips with a napkin, then placed it in her lap. "So this *is* Teeleh's castle?"

"Oh yes. It's exquisite, isn't it? Perfectly lovely and charming, just like Teeleh."

Theo and Annelee exchanged glances.

Rosaline continued. "I can't wait to officially join my life to his. It can't happen soon enough. Just as soon as I'm free of … oh, what's his name?" She waved her hand through the air.

"William," Annelee replied.

"Oh yeah." Rosaline laughed. "I can't believe I almost forgot."

"You did forget," Theo said.

"Well, that's what happens when you're in love," Rosaline said. "You forget all about your past. The only thing that matters is your betrothed."

"William is your betrothed," Annelee said. But once again, Rosaline seemed not to hear her.

"Where is Teeleh?" Theo asked.

"Oh, he'll come join us when he's good and ready. He lives under the law of no man." She smiled and stabbed a piece of fish with her fork. "It's one of the things I love about him." She popped the bite into her mouth. "That and the fact that he absolutely adores me. In fact, he loves me so much, he'd never let me leave."

"That sounds like a prison," Theo said.

"Oh no," Rosaline waved his words away and smiled. "If I wanted to leave, I could. I'd just have to ask him. Surely, he'd allow me to. But why would I?"

"So he's not holding you hostage?" Annelee asked.

"What a funny thing to ask." Rosaline wrinkled her nose. "I mean, I suppose you could say it started out that way. But that's only because I didn't know Teeleh yet. Now, I never want to leave."

"Something isn't right with her," Theo whispered to Annelee.

"You're telling me."

"Darling," Rosaline motioned to Theo. "You haven't touched your plate. Would you like some mint jelly for that lamb?"

Theo glanced down at his plate. Though his stomach

roared with hunger, his mind was too distracted with the new clues Rosaline was feeding him.

"Uh, my dad always made it with fig jam. Do you have any figs?"

A loud clatter filled the dining room as Rosaline dropped her fork against her plate. "Oh, forgive me." She picked it up and placed it beside her drinking glass. "No, no figs, I'm afraid."

"Plums then?" Theo asked. "Or perhaps a date?" He glanced up and down the table at the decadent spread, noticing for the first time that not a single piece of fruit adorned the table.

"Any fruit jam would do," he added. "Blackberry, perhaps?"

"Oh," Rosaline smoothed her hands over her dress. "No. No fruit. None in the whole house, in fact."

Theo sensed hesitation in her voice.

"Why?" he asked.

Rosaline dabbed her mouth with her napkin, leaned forward, and lowered her voice. "Because fruit, when eaten, gives great power. And power belongs only to Teeleh."

Silence followed her words.

"Oh!" Rosaline pushed back from the table and stood as if suddenly remembering something. "But we do have pie! Pecan pie, of course." She gathered her dress and darted through the door in the back wall toward the kitchen.

As soon as the door swung shut behind her, Annelee turned to Theo and said, "We need to get out of here, and we need to take her with us."

"I don't think she'll leave. You heard her. She's in love with Teeleh. Besides, we can't leave without the book."

"I cannot fathom how or why she's fallen in love with that beast." Annelee pushed back from the table but didn't stand. "If he's anything like that monster Marsuuv ..."

A door creaked open behind them. Theo turned to see a man enter from the hallway.

A small gasp escaped Annelee's lips when she turned to see what had caught Theo's attention.

A statuesque man glided into the room. Dressed in an ivory-colored three-piece suit with a red rose boutonniere, there was no mistaking him.

"Teeleh," Theo whispered. Or at least, he thought he had. But his voice didn't make a sound.

With a hand in each pocket, the man stopped just inside the dining room door. Golden eyes stared back at Theo, the same color as the man's hair. His striking features looked like they'd been carved from marble.

And suddenly Theo could understand why Rosaline had fallen in love with Teeleh. He looked more like a prince than handsome William.

"Hello, Theodore." Teeleh dipped his head. "And Annelee." He spoke in a smooth baritone. "I see my future queen has provided you with some refreshments after your long journey. I do hope you're feeling revived."

"Yes, thank you," Annelee said.

Theo detected an odd tone in her voice.

"Ah, ah, ah. No need for that," Teeleh said, golden eyes fixed on Annelee.

Theo felt her stiffen beside him, then realized she'd been reaching for her bow under the table. Theo hadn't even seen her flinch. He wondered how Teeleh knew.

"The same way I know anything, Theo," Teeleh said with a beguiling smile. "Now, if Annelee wouldn't mind putting away her weapon." He paused and waited.

Annelee folded her empty hands in her lap.

"Very good. Now, I don't know what you've heard about me, but I assure you, you're not in any harm or trouble. I've invited you here as my guests."

Theo started to speak when Rosaline re-entered the room.

"Oh, darling! You're here!" She started toward him, but he held up a hand. Rosaline froze. "Oh. Forgive me. I forget myself."

"It's quite all right, my dear. I've simply come to welcome our guests."

"Yes, of course." She fidgeted with her dress. "They're

lovely, aren't they? It's been so long since I've hosted guests. Oh!" Her hands flew to her mouth. "I know! Can we throw a party? A ball, perhaps? Oh, please say yes, darling!"

"You may do whatever you wish, my love. This is your home too. If it pleases you, then throw a ball. In fact, why not tonight? Our guests can join us. After all, we have much to celebrate." He flashed Rosaline a charming smile.

The princess rushed over to the table and flopped down into the seat nearest Annelee. She grabbed her hands and leaned forward. "You will come to my ball, won't you?"

Annelee shot Theo a look, swallowed, then said, "Of course, Princess."

Rosaline squeezed Annelee's hands, then jumped up from the table.

"Darling?" Teeleh said.

"Yes, my love?"

"Before you get caught up with your preparations, will you please show our guests to their rooms? They must be exhausted. I believe an afternoon respite is in order before tonight's festivities."

"Oh, yes of course."

Teeleh locked eyes with Theo. "It's my honor to host you in my home. I do hope you enjoy your stay."

He dipped his head, smiled, then took his leave from the room.

.

Chapter Seven

THEO SAT ON THE END of the ornate four-poster bed in his private chambers inside Teeleh's castle, staring at a painting on the opposite wall. Late-afternoon sunlight streamed in through the cracks of the heavy velvet drapes, which matched the linens on the bed. He'd been sitting there for hours, locked in by Rosaline.

After finishing their meal, the princess had first shown Annelee to her room, then Theo to his, one door down. He'd stepped inside to examine the elaborate furnishings when the door had swung closed behind him and the lock clicked into place.

Three times Theo had called out to Rosaline, but if she heard him, she didn't acknowledge it. He soon realized the young princess had likely rushed off to plan for her ball, more occupied with the arrangements than with the guests who'd be attending.

After trying unsuccessfully to communicate with Annelee through the adjoining wall of their rooms, Theo had finally given up and taken a seat on the end of the bed, eyes tracing the textured smears of oil paints that coated the canvas and formed a classic still-life painting of a bowl of fruit. The irony didn't escape him.

"Fruit," he mumbled to himself, thinking back to what Sebastian had said about the fruit of the Dark Forest. Theo blinked. He'd nearly forgotten they were inside the Dark Forest.

"Theo is Theo," he said, while sinking deeper into his thoughts. "White, green, black, red, and white." He chewed his lip, allowing his mind to swirl with ideas, forcing his brain to make the connections he knew were there but wasn't seeing. "Remember," he said, as if coaching himself. Then more harshly, "Remember!"

With a sigh of frustration, he flopped back onto the bed and closed his eyes.

A now familiar image of a book filled his mind. He imagined himself flipping open its worn leather cover, thumbing through the blank pages until he spotted the one with four reddish-brown stains.

"Red," he said to himself. "Surrender." But even as he said it, he didn't understand what it meant.

He lay there for several minutes, eyes closed, silently working through the clues in his mind. He paused only when he heard a loud *click* echo through the room.

Theo's eyes flew open. He sat up and stared at the bedroom door as it groaned open, stopping after a few inches. He waited for someone to enter.

No one did.

He rubbed his eyes and proceeded to wait a few more seconds. When no one appeared, he stood and crossed to the door, pulled it open the rest of the way, and peered out into the hallway.

"Hello?" Theo called. Only his echo replied from the empty hallway.

He listened for several seconds, waiting to hear a door close down the hall or the sound of footsteps fading into the distance, any sign of the mysterious person who'd unlocked his door.

"This doesn't feel right," he said to himself, feet hesitating on the threshold.

He chewed his lip and stared into the hallway, unable to ignore the pull of curiosity that demanded he wander away from his room and explore the halls of Teeleh's castle. After all, he had a book to find.

"It has to be a trap," he said to himself.

"Yes, but I won't fall for it," he whispered, as if in reply.

"But what if I do?" he asked, continuing the conversation with himself.

"I won't. I'm far too intelligent for that."

"Okay, but be careful," he warned himself, then slipped into the hallway.

A wave of excitement rushed through him as his footfalls echoed through the ornate hall. Yes, he was far too intelligent to fall for the trap—especially because he *knew* it was a trap. But he also felt entirely certain that though this castle may hold his demise, it also held answers—truths Theo had to discover. And those truths would be in a book.

"Theo is Theo," he mumbled to himself as he darted down the hall, still not fully knowing what it meant but certain he'd find out.

Annelee sat on the end of the bed in her room, staring at a peculiar but well-executed oil painting of a bowl of fruit. She found it odd, considering what Princess Rosaline had shared with them during their lunch about fruit. She flopped back onto the bed and folded her arms over chest, wishing she had her bow. Unfortunately, Rosaline had taken it when she'd locked Annelee inside the bedchamber.

Instead, she reached for the journal on the bed beside her and reread the strange words she'd scribbled onto the pages.

"Theo is Theo," she whispered while picturing him as her strong comrade in William's army, not the thin, red-headed young man she traveled with now. She wished Theo the warrior was with her, feeling confident that together, they could surely defeat Teeleh and escape with Rosaline and the mysterious book. Instead, she was stuck with Theo the nerd, who talked to himself and said things that didn't make sense.

She sighed, sat up, and glanced around the room, having already searched it for any sign of a book. She closed the journal and tucked it back inside her satchel, unable to shake the feeling that something was very wrong with their whole situation.

Especially concerning Rosaline.

A loud *click* filled the room.

Annelee glanced over at the bedroom door. It glided open, but no one entered.

Standing, Annelee swung her satchel over her shoulder. "Rosaline?"

No response.

"Is that you?"

Annelee peeked her head out the door and scanned the empty hallway. The bedroom door next to her room stood open.

"Theo?"

She glanced both ways, then slipped down the hall, remembering that Rosaline had said Theo would be in the room next to hers. She darted inside when she reached it.

"Theo?"

But the room was empty.

Annelee stood in the center of the bedchamber for a long moment, noting that the room was a mirrored image of hers, right down to the painting of fruit. She stared at it for a long second before darting back out into the hall.

"Theo!" she called in a loud whisper, trying to ignore the sinking feeling in her stomach. He'd gone off in search of the book, she knew it. But she also knew without a doubt in her bones that this was a trap.

And Theo was just smart enough to fall for it.

Theo spent nearly an hour wandering the castle in search of a book, and despite checking all the obvious places, he found nothing and saw no one. Silence lingered in the halls, making him more uncomfortable with every passing second. But still, he couldn't fight the uncontrollable curiosity to continue his search.

"Theo is Theo," he mumbled as he rounded a corner and entered another hall of the sprawling castle.

He peered inside each open doorway as he passed,

knowing Teeleh was too smart to leave a special book in a place as obvious as a study or a library. He had to find the most secret place, a hidden room or mysterious cubby. Somewhere Teeleh wouldn't expect anyone else to look.

He quickened his pace as he traveled the length of the red-and-white-tiled hall.

"Red," Theo said. "Surrender. White. The light is infinite."

He shook his head, still having no clue what the words meant but unable to ignore them. He picked up his pace again, this time jogging down the hall, passing room after room, no longer looking inside.

The pounding of his feet synced with the beat of his heart, making his own pulse sound impossibly loud in the cavernous halls of the castle. After several more minutes of rounding corners and jogging down tiled floors, Theo stopped, disoriented and finally ready to give up the search and return to his room.

But the pounding sound continued.

Theo froze and listened.

The rhythmic beat had not been his footfalls or his pulse.

He turned and faced the end of the hall, realizing the sound came from that direction, from a closed door at the end.

The thrum pulsed like a heartbeat behind the closed door.

Theo rushed down the corridor, once again pulled by an irresistible curiosity. He paused with his hand on the doorknob, feeling the beat through the cool metal. He twisted it, then pushed the door inward and stepped inside a vast round room.

The sound of the pulse softened as he walked the perimeter. Towering windows lined the walls, framed with yards of red velvet curtains that draped from ceiling to floor, each one interspaced with paintings of a strange land. Theo paused in front of one of them, his eyes tracing the white dunes of a desert. The next featured a vibrant green lake. The picture stirred Theo's mind. When he saw a playground on a beach, he grabbed his temples. The next image, a lion made of sand, caused him to squeeze his eyes shut. The gentle thrum of the room pulsed against his eardrums.

"Remember," Theo said, feeling certain he had all the clues, though he couldn't piece them together.

He opened his eyes and scanned the round room, realizing as he glimpsed the view from the windows that he stood in the centermost tower of the castle.

"The center," he said. "The heart."

He glanced down at the floor, noticing for the first time that the red and white tiles formed a different design in here. White tiles lined the perimeter of the round room, allowing the red to form a distinct image on the middle of the floor. Theo stepped into the center, standing directly on top of a giant, red-tile heart.

A thrum pulsed beneath his feet.

"I'm in the heart of the castle," he said. "The heart of the Dark Forest."

He stooped and touched a hand to the cool floor, feeling the heartbeat grow stronger. The curiosity swelled inside him, now feeling insatiable.

"The book has to be close." He stood and searched the room, glancing again at every painting and velvet-framed window. He paused. The curtains were drawn over one of the windows, and the bottom corner of fabric bunched along the floor, exposing a sliver of dark wood. Theo crossed the room and drew back the curtain, revealing not a window but a door. The pulse-like beat hammered from the other side.

Theo hesitated. "This could still be a trap," he said to himself.

But even as he said it, the heartbeat summoned him. He recalled Marsuuv's claim that he and Annelee would find the book in the heart of the Dark Forest. And Sebastian's words—that Teeleh's castle was the heart of this strange land.

"And this is the heart of the heart," Theo said. He

wrapped his fingers around the doorknob, twisted, and pulled. Darkness greeted him. But after a few seconds of staring through the doorway, he came to see a faint light from below illuminating a spiral staircase. The heartbeat continued to pulse, drawing him through the door and down the winding stairs until his booted feet touched down on a stone floor.

Theo scanned the dimly lit room. Empty bookcases lined the round walls, each one covered with a thin layer of dust. Hanging from the low ceiling in the center, a small chandelier glinted with candlelight, illuminating the main feature of the room—a pedestal topped with a glass bell jar. Inside: one piece of bright-green fruit.

Theo crossed the room and paused in front of it, watching as the fruit hovered in the air beneath the glass, gently rotating clockwise.

His mind came alive at the sight of it.

"Green," he said.

His thoughts raced through the events of the past few days: meeting Annelee, learning of their strange connection, Marsuuv's insistence that the two of them were not from this world, Sebastian, the Shataiki, Rosaline and what she'd told them about fruit …

"Green …"

He reached out a tentative hand and touched the

cool jar. The heartbeat pulsed against the glass as if it were coming from the fruit itself.

He lifted the bell jar and watched the fruit slowly turn.

"Green like water," he said, recalling the picture of the green lake in the room directly above him. "Green like life." He snatched the fruit from the air. "Green like ... like ..." The words lingered on the tip of his tongue. He squeezed his eyes shut. "Remember. Remember!"

The sound of footsteps echoed above him. Theo's eyes flew open. He stared at the piece of fruit in his hand.

"This has to be it," he said to himself. "This fruit has to be the answer."

After all, Sebastian had told him of the power of the fruit inside the Dark Forest. And Rosaline had confirmed it, even saying that its power belonged only to Teeleh.

The fruit had to be the answer—to give Theo power and help him remember.

The footsteps above shifted, and Theo could tell they moved toward the spiral staircase behind the curtain.

He clenched the soft flesh of the fruit between his fingers, feeling drawn to its sweet smell.

"But is this too easy?" he asked himself. "Is it a trap?"

His mind spun through all the disjointed pieces of information as he heard the footsteps descend the stairs. He glanced behind him, unable to see who it was, then turned his attention back to the fruit.

"No," he breathed. "This is it. I know it is."

In his mind, he flipped through the clues one more time, landing on the only action that made sense.

"I have to eat the fruit."

Annelee stepped into the strange round room, noting immediately the red-tile heart on the center of the floor. "The heart," she said as she closed the door behind her. "Theo?" she called to him in a loud whisper, feeling certain he had to be close. But another sensation overtook her as she stepped into the center of the room—dread.

"Theo?"

She walked the perimeter of the room, pausing to glance through each window and stare at each painting. A few of the images felt familiar.

She froze when she came upon an open door. A gust of cool air exhaled over her body. Faint light flickered from below.

She swallowed, once again wishing she had her bow,

and descended the wooden spiral staircase. With every step, her dread intensified, along with the unsettling certainty that she'd find Theo at the bottom.

She saw him as her foot hit the last step.

He stood in the center of the round stone room, holding a piece of bright-green fruit.

Everything inside her screamed at him to stop, but she couldn't get the words out fast enough.

"Theo! Don't!"

When he turned to face her, she realized she was too late.

He flashed her an overly confident smile as juice ran down his chin.

Chapter Eight

THEO STARED AT ANNELEE, feeling the juice of the fruit drip down his face. His vision blurred for a few seconds, then cleared, as did his mind. His thoughts fogged over as if he were suddenly forgetting where he was, *who* he was. Then everything snapped into focus.

"Whoa," he said, wonder filling his words. "This is incredible."

"Theo, what did you do?" Annelee jerked the fruit from his hand and placed it on the stone pedestal. "Sebastian warned us not to eat any fruit."

Theo started to answer her, then stopped. All around him, the room divided into pieces, as if he was able to see behind the veil of the physical realm into the energetic workings of each atom that made up the space. His brain unlocked, intoxicating him with the power of his own intellect. He felt like he could solve any problem and see all possibilities.

"This is amazing," he said, facing Annelee. "I under-stand now. I finally get it."

"You finally get it? Theo …" She touched his hand. "What are you talking about?"

"I solved it," he said. "I solved the game."

"What game?"

"This game." He gestured around the room. "It's all just a puzzle."

Annelee shook her head. "I have a bad feeling about this."

"You see, that's your problem," he said. "You think with your feelings instead of your mind." He tapped the side of his head. "But all we need is our intellect, our intelligence. Here." He picked up the fruit and handed it to her.

"No." She took the fruit from his hand and slammed it back down onto the stone surface. It splattered and sprayed him with pulp.

"I know where the book is," Theo said.

She paused. "You do?"

"Yes."

"How?"

"Because I'm thinking with my head, not with my heart. Don't you get it?"

Annelee shook her head. "No. You sound crazy."

"Intellect is crazy to those who don't understand."

She just stared at him.

"Follow me," he said as he started up the spiral staircase.

Annelee followed close behind.

When he reached the top, he pushed aside the thick red velvet curtain and stepped into the center of the room. Teeleh and Rosaline stood waiting for them, just as Theo expected.

"Well done," Teeleh said. "I see you found my fruit."

Theo nodded. "I did. And now I can see the truth."

"Can you now? Then you'll not be surprised by this ..."

He snapped his fingers and two large Shataiki entered, dragging a bloodied and beaten William between them.

"Rosaline!" William gasped.

"William!" Annelee rushed toward her commanding officer. But two more Shataiki appeared and apprehended her.

The beasts holding William tightened their grip.

Theo cast a quick glance back at Annelee but remained unfazed.

"I know you have the book," Theo said, facing Teeleh again.

The man's smile gleamed in the late-afternoon light

that streamed through the windows. He reached into the inner pocket of his suit jacket and pulled out a leather-bound book. Theo's mind pulsed with memories.

"The Book of History," he said.

"Correct, young man. Well done. You've found it."

"Rosaline! Are you hurt?" William asked, but the princess hardly looked at him. "What have you done to her?" William demanded.

"I've done nothing," Teeleh said. "She merely sees the truth now. As do you," he said to Theo.

"What's he talking about, Theo?" Annelee asked, confusion evident in her voice.

"Do you want to tell her or should I?" Teeleh grinned.

"I have something to say," Rosaline interjected.

William stared at her, a flicker of hope lingering in his eyes.

"Go on, darling," Teeleh said.

She released Teeleh's arm and crossed the room to where William knelt, a Shataiki holding up each of his arms.

She crouched in front of him, lowering her face toward his.

"Rosaline, my love. I have not stopped pursuing you since the moment you went missing."

"Shhh ..." She pressed a finger to his lips. "William..."

"Yes, my love?"

She stroked his cheek. "You are nothing to me now."

The hope on the prince's face shattered.

"I formally renounce my betrothal to you," she said as she stood, then returned to Teeleh's side. "This man is to be my husband now." She looped her arm through Teeleh's and peered up at him with a wide grin.

A wail escaped William's lips. He collapsed under the weight of his own grief, falling to the floor with shoulder-racking sobs. The Shataiki released him, leaving him to his misery. William's wails shifted to a scream. "Teeleh!" he shouted.

The man smoothed his suit jacket and turned to look at the prince.

"End me!" William demanded. "Put me out of my misery now!"

Teeleh stared at him for only a moment, then said. "No."

"Why?" William gasped. "I thought you wanted me dead. I'm begging you. Finish what you've started. I am nothing without Rosaline. Why keep me alive?"

"You'll receive your answers in due time, Prince."

"Theo!" Annelee shouted, still bound by the other two black bats. "Do something!"

Teeleh took a step toward Theo. "Yes, Theo. It's time for you to do something."

Theo glanced from Rosaline to William to Annelee,

his mind swirling and snapping as he considered every possibility and each outcome. But he'd already worked through each of them half a dozen times, his synapses firing at an impossible speed. And once again, he came to the same conclusion. He stared at the floor, eyes tracing the red-tile heart in the center of the room.

"This is the end," he said.

Teeleh nodded. "I see you truly are a man of reason and logic. Perhaps, now more than ever, thanks to my little secret you discovered." He gestured to the sticky green-fruit residue that lingered on Theo's chin.

Theo wiped it with the back of his arm. A burning sensation fired on his shoulder as he did, and for the first time since entering Teeleh's castle, Theo remembered the black bars that marked his arm—the supposed curse that had appeared around the same time his father committed himself to Marsuuv and his Dark Riders.

Was that man even his real father?

"I'm not from this world," Theo said, remembering Marsuuv's words.

Teeleh nodded. "Correct, Dream Traveler."

The phrase sent a shiver through Theo's bones. "Dream Traveler," he repeated, his mind reworking the puzzle pieces once again to make sure he didn't miss anything. "It's a game. An illusion."

Teeleh cocked his head. When Theo didn't continue, he said, "Come here, and let me see your hands."

"Theo!" Annelee shouted, but one of the Shataiki clamped a winged hand over her mouth.

Theo stepped closer to Teeleh and held up both of his hands. Teeleh examined them carefully, lingering over every dried scrape and cut. When he seemed satisfied with his inspection, he simply said, "Good," and handed Theo the Book of History. He reached into his breast pocket and produced a quill. "Now, I'd like you to do me a little favor. You see, your words hold great power. Some have even said that one such as yourself can write things into existence."

Theo opened the book and flipped through the pages. Strange characters lined the aged parchment, filling the book with a language he'd never seen before. And yet … it was also familiar.

A loud screech filled the room.

Theo spun around to see that Annelee had stomped on the foot of one of the Shataiki. It released its hand from her mouth.

"Theo! Don't!"

The wounded Shataiki recovered and gripped her tighter than before.

"Don't do a thing he says!" she screamed. "Can't you feel it? This is a trap!"

Theo glanced back down at the book in his hands, noticing the way certain characters in the strange language repeated. A predictable pattern emerged.

"It's a code," Theo said. "A code book."

Teeleh shrugged. "I prefer to think of it as a book of life here in this world. But yes, a code book, so to speak."

Theo flipped to the end, finding several blank pages at the back of the book.

"And you, Dream Traveler, can change the code."

Theo peered up at Teeleh. A sinking feeling formed in his gut. His mind pulled the puzzle pieces together. "You're trapped here. You want me to release you from the Dark Forest."

"How astute of you. But then again, you are using that brilliant brain of yours." Teeleh tapped his temple. "Yes, break my bond to this cursed forest. Release me from my prison. Write it, and it will be so. Then, I'll let you go."

"Theo! Don't!" Annelee screamed again.

Theo took the quill from Teeleh's hand. His mind spun through all the possibilities once more, but this time it came to a screeching halt. "This is the end," he whispered, understanding the words on a different level. He turned to face Annelee. "I have to do this," he said. "It's the only way."

"Listen to me, Theo," Annelee said. "Put aside your

logic. Use your heart."

Theo flipped back through the code-filled pages, hoping they'd reveal to him any other path than the one that lay before him. He traced a finger over the mysterious characters.

"Use your heart, Theo!" Annelee shouted again.

A warm feeling spread through Theo's chest as he flipped back to the blank pages at the end of the book. "You don't understand," Theo said, looking up at her. "I am using my heart."

Annelee's voice quivered. "What do you mean?"

Theo gripped the quill in his hand, hovering the tip over one of the blank pages. "I can see all options, all possibilities, all outcomes …"

"Then don't do this," Annelee said, her voice barely above a whisper.

"You still don't get it," Theo said. "He's already won. This is the only way."

"The only way for what?"

He didn't answer.

Tears welled in her eyes. "Find a book," she said. "Rescue the princess. Save Viren. Remember?"

The word *remember* lodged in his mind.

Life is a cycle of remembering and forgetting.

Theo dropped the quill onto the open page of the book and gripped the side of his head in frustration, disturbed by a truth deeper than his intellect. Staring at the tile heart on the floor, he tried to force himself to make sense of it, but he couldn't see beyond the matrix of his current reality, which unfolded before his eyes like a beautiful tapestry.

"Theo is Theo," Annelee said. "Find a book, rescue the princess, and save—"

"No!" Theo shook his head and dropped his hand. "We can't." He ran a finger over the blank page. "No matter what we do, Teeleh wins. But this is how we get out of the game, by ending it. This is the only way."

"It's not the only way!" Annelee protested.

"Yes!" Theo shouted. "Yes, it is! This is the only way you don't die!"

Annelee stumbled back as if the air had been sucked from her lungs.

"I am using my heart," Theo said in a near whisper, then before Annelee could say another word, he sucked in a deep breath, picked up the quill, and scribbled a quick sentence onto the blank page.

The Dark Forest's bonds over Teeleh are broken.

The words glowed with a hot light.

"One more thing," Teeleh said. "Write that my freedom cannot be revoked."

Theo wrote the addendum beneath the first sentence.

A menacing chuckle escaped Teeleh's lips. He snatched the book from Theo's hands. But when Theo peered up at him, he was no longer a man.

An eight-foot-tall Shataiki stood in Teeleh's place, gripping the Book of History in his winged hand. "Thank you, Theo," he said in a gravelly voice, then turned to face William. "As for you, Prince, you're wondering why I don't kill you?" The giant Shataiki leaned down and snarled in William's face. "It's because I don't need to. You're no longer a threat. I have your princess and your kingdom. And now, thanks to my precious little pet"—he turned to stare at Rosaline— "I'll have the devotion of all the citizens of Viren. Once they see how she loves me, they'll love me too. And eventually, they'll worship me."

Rosaline trembled as she stared at him.

Teeleh stood. "What is it, darling? Don't you love me now in my true form?"

Rosaline's voice quivered. "No, I … I do. It's just that … I'll have to adjust to …"

"Save your words," Teeleh growled. "After all, they hold no power." He returned his attention to William. "And neither do you. You have no power, no kingdom, no princess, no crown. I've stolen everything from you. And *no*, I will not end your misery. I'll leave you to wallow in it. I am the lord of suffering, and now you've seen a glimpse of what it will look like to live under my reign." Spittle flew from his mouth as he laughed.

Teeleh turned to faced Theo. "And you have this brilliant boy to thank. Yes, the prince was my original target. After all, his betrothal to Rosaline stood in the way of my marriage to her—a union that is necessary to win the hearts of the people. But what I didn't yet know was how I'd rid myself of these invisible chains to this dreaded forest, that is until my servant Marsuuv caught wind of a boy with unique power, a boy who is not from this world ..." Teeleh narrowed his red Shataiki stare. "Your arrival changed the game, Theo. You've given me the keys to the kingdom. And for that, I thank you."

Teeleh stretched out his massive wings, then snatched Rosaline up in his taloned feet and burst through one of the windows.

Broken glass crunched beneath Theo's boots as he rushed to the window to watch the giant beast fly through the sky, the princess held in his clutches. He ducked as two smaller Shataiki flew past him and out the window. Then two more.

Feeling suddenly faint, Theo collapsed onto the ground.

Annelee, now free, rushed to his side. "Theo?" She shook his shoulders. "Theo?"

His head slumped. His mind clouded over.

"Theo?" Annelee slapped his cheek.

The sound of William's wails pulled Theo from his stupor. The fog in his mind dissipated, leaving behind a searing headache. His eyes fell on the shattered prince, who crouched on the floor in a puddle of tears. He wanted to reassure William that all would be okay, but Theo could no longer see all possibilities and outcomes. The effects of the fruit were gone.

Now he was just Theo.

He shook his head, disgusted by what he'd done, though he'd had no other option.

Annelee helped him to his feet and together they stared out the window, watching the sky darken with hordes of Shataiki as they fled the castle, blanketing the sky and blocking out the light of the sun.

Theo didn't need a special fruit to know where they were headed.

They were going to Viren to witness their master's wedding.

Chapter Nine

THEO COLLAPSED onto the floor beneath the window, unable to watch the horrible events he'd set into motion. With the effects of the fruit now gone, he felt faint and weary. His stomach churned with the memory of what he'd been able to see just moments before, the ripple effects of his actions that would soon take place.

Annelee slid to the floor beside him and stared straight ahead.

"Please forgive me," Theo said. "I ate the fruit. It was a mistake. It opened my eyes and my mind to consequences I never could've seen on my own. Perhaps, if I hadn't eaten it, I would've chosen another way. Maybe I would've even won." He paused, then turned to face her. "But you wouldn't have."

She turned to look at him, her face unreadable. "All this talk of a game and winning, it doesn't make sense.

You're too smart for your own good. I told you to use your heart not your mind."

"And I told you that I did."

She pressed her lips together, then said, "I really would have died?"

He reached for her hand. She didn't pull away. Staring down at their joined fingers he said, "In every scenario but this one." He peered into her eyes. "This was the only one where you lived."

Annelee's lips parted as if she were about to speak, but Theo continued. "And keeping you alive felt like a win to me."

Theo watched as Annelee blinked back tears. She squeezed his hand, then stood.

"Where are you going?" he asked.

She held out a hand and yanked Theo to his feet.

"*We* are going to stop a wedding."

Theo shook his head. "We can't. It's impossible. It's over."

Annelee pulled up her sleeve, exposing three full black bars on her shoulder. "It's not over." She tapped the marks. "And forget about what's possible and what's not." She grinned. "Because we're not from this world."

"What are you saying?" Theo asked.

"And I thought you were the smart one." Annelee snickered. "You said the fruit made you see all options, all possibilities, right?"

"Right," Theo said.

"But that's only what's possible in this world …"

Something deep inside Theo's soul clicked into place.

"And we're not from this world," he said. "You're right. We have to try to stop the wedding."

"Now that's the Theo I know." She flashed him a grin, then wrapped him in a tight hug.

Theo breathed in her scent: fresh air, sunshine, and strawberries. The smell overwhelmed his mind with images, with memories …

Life is a cycle of remembering and forgetting.

A loud groan interrupted the moment. Theo pulled away from Annelee to see William crouched on the tiled floor. The man looked as if he'd been through a battle and lost.

"William, are you okay?" Annelee rushed to his side. She tried to pull him to his feet, but he resisted. "Where are the others?" she asked. "Conrad, Elijah, Liam?"

"I had to leave them. They never would've allowed me to come here."

"All the more reason to take you with us. C'mon, we need to get you moving."

"Leave me, Hawk." He pushed her away.

She grabbed his arm and tugged. "You're my

commanding officer. I will not leave you. Besides, we need to hurry if we're going to stop the wedding. You know as well as I do that King Tyrus must perform the ceremony. We need to get to him before—"

"I said leave me!"

William's voice echoed with a loud boom.

Annelee dropped his arm.

"Didn't you see the way Rosaline looked at me?" William gasped. "Didn't you hear what she said? She said I am nothing to her." His voice cracked.

"Forget what she said." Annelee grabbed his arm again. "Rosaline is under Teeleh's spell, just as Theo was. Now stand up."

William wiped his eyes with the back of his hand and rose to his knees. He peered up at her. "If there is any hope for me and Rosaline, it lies with you, Hawk. You're one of the bravest and strongest warriors I've ever fought with." He stared at her for a long moment, clarity washing over his face. "I thought you were dead."

Annelee smiled. "You can't be rid of me that easily."

He nodded, but his face darkened. "What of Wolf, your friend? Did he make it through the battle with his life?"

Annelee stood. "Barely," she said. She crossed the room and approached Theo. Taking him by the hand, she pulled him over to meet William.

"William, I'd like you to meet Theo."

"Theo?" he said. "Another Theo?"

Annelee laughed. "No, Theo *is* Theo."

William rubbed his forehead. "Your words don't make sense. Now, go on. Leave me here."

"He's right," Annelee said to Theo. "If there's any hope of reaching Viren before the wedding, we need to go now. There's just one last thing."

"What's that?" Theo asked.

Annelee reached over and lifted the sleeve of his shirt.

Only one full black bar remained on Theo's shoulder.

She winced and pulled the sleeve back into place. "Don't you dare use your intellect again. You'll drain the rest of your life force. And besides," she grinned. "I like you better when you think with your heart. Now, c'mon. We need to get to our horses and my bow."

She pulled him by the arm toward the door that led back into the halls of Teeleh's castle. Before following her out of the room, Theo cast a final glance back at William. He sat with his knees drawn to his chest, staring at the floor with a blank expression.

"We'll rescue her," Theo called back to him. "We'll rescue the princess from that monster."

William glanced up.

"And after we do that," Theo said, "we'll find a way to save the Kingdom of Viren."

Chapter Ten

THEO GRIPPED THE REINS of his horse tighter. The animal's muscles tensed and quivered beneath his legs as it galloped between the trees of the Dark Forest. Both he and Annelee had pushed the horses harder than either of them had ever ridden before, stopping only for short breaks and riding straight through the night. They'd covered the distance from Teeleh's castle back to the Emerald River in record time, but Theo worried it still wouldn't be fast enough.

He glanced at Annelee, who leaned over the neck of her horse, knuckles blanching as she clung to its reins. Foam dotted its lips. She caught Theo's eye and shouted, "We're almost there!" He wondered if she could read the exhaustion on his face. Faintness washed over him as he clung to the horse, knowing his life force must be dangerously low.

Less than ten minutes later, they burst through the

tree line of the Dark Forest and jerked the horses to a stop at the bank of the Emerald River. Its deep-green waters glimmered in the midday sunlight.

Annelee gasped as she stared across the waterway. "Look!" she pointed. "The forests of Viren, they're …"

"Dead." Theo rolled off his horse and stared across the river at the blackened trees. The once lush woods of Viren now stood as an extension of the Dark Forest.

He tried to pull himself to his feet but couldn't stand.

"Let me help you." Annelee rushed to his side, but Theo waved her away.

"I can't," he said.

"You have to."

"I can't!"

"You have to try!"

Theo pushed up his sleeve and showed her his arm. "I have a quarter of a bar left, and it's still a two-day ride to the city. I'll never make it."

Annelee examined her own arm. She, too, had lost three-quarters of a bar during their race from Teeleh's castle.

"I'll find a Waystation and get you to it—even if you collapse. I've done it once before."

"There are no more Waystations!" Theo shouted, not knowing how he knew it. He softened his tone. "Even if there were, there's no way you could get me to one and still make it to the city before the wedding takes place. That's if it hasn't already happened. You have to go without me."

"Absolutely not."

"You have to."

"I won't."

"Then we lose!"

Annelee knelt beside him and grabbed his hand. She leaned in and stared straight into his eyes. "Theo, I don't understand what you mean when you say we're playing a game. But let me put this into words I think you'll understand. Either we *win* together, or we *lose* together. It's my turn to think with my heart, and I'm not leaving you." She touched her chest. "Theo is Theo. I don't know how I know this, but I *know* it. I know you." She held his gaze for a long moment. "You're my Theo."

Warmth spread through his body at the sound of her words. "You'd make that sacrifice for me?"

"I *am* making this sacrifice for you," she said.

"But what about—" Theo stopped midsentence.

"What about what?" she asked.

"Sacrifice," Theo mumbled. "Surrender. Red."

"Stop," Annelee commanded. "Stop trying to puzzle it all out. You'll drain your life force even faster."

"Red," Theo said, unable to stop himself. "Sacrifice. Surrender."

"Stop it, Theo. Stop using your mind."

He shook his head and crawled toward the edge of the river. "I'm not using my mind." He stared into the clear green waters. "I'm using my heart."

Images flashed through Theo's brain, each one stirring a knowing in the deepest parts of him.

"How'd I know what a Shataiki looked like?" he asked his reflection. "How'd I know about the Waystations? How'd I know you?" He glanced over his shoulder at Annelee. "And how'd I know that Theo is Theo?"

She tossed her hands into the air. "Because I wrote it in my journal. Now, please stop."

Theo turned back to his reflection. "White," he said. "Green, black, red, and white."

He heard Annelee approach. Her voice sounded softer this time. "Those are the colors from my journal."

"Right." He dipped a finger into the water. "I know what they mean."

"You do? How?"

Theo smiled at his reflection. "Because I remember."

He plunged his whole hand into the water. A rush of energy flowed up his arm and awakened his mind.

A green lake.

A boy with blue eyes who stood on the shore, crafting lions made of sand.

Hyenas that couldn't threaten him.

Fears that couldn't overtake him.

Love that filled him.
And friends who surrounded him.

"Life is a cycle of remembering and forgetting," Theo said as he brought his awareness back to the present moment. He touched his left hand to his right shoulder and the thin strip of a bar that remained. "White: the light is infinite. Black: we're blind in this world. Red: surrender. And white: love."

Annelee knelt on the riverbank beside him. "You skipped green. What does it mean?"

"We are the light of the world." Theo smiled at her. "And we're not from this world."

She shook her head. "I still don't understand."

"We're not from this world, just in it, like avatars in a game, having an experience to teach us something—to teach us to remember."

"To remember what?" she asked.

"Who we really are." He grinned. "Theo is Theo."

His entire body burst with warmth as he said it, finally understanding the true meaning of the words for the first time.

A new wave of memories flooded him.

"I'm not Theo the Bard," he said.

Annelee's eyes flickered with recognition as he said it.

"I'm not Theo the Warrior."

A smile tugged at her lips.

"And I'm not Theo the Savant."

"You're Theo," she said. "Theo is Theo."

"And Annelee is Annelee."

She nodded, her expression shifting to one of clarity and joy. "I'm not Annelee the Herbalist or the Archer. I'm Annelee, the light of the world."

"Exactly. And the only way for us to reveal that light is to remove the things that block it."

"Which are?"

"Our avatars." Theo dipped his left hand into the river, feeling the cool water glide across his skin. He remembered swimming through green waters like these once before, breathing in the intoxicating liquid that filled him with love—the evidence of being in the light.

"This is a game," he said. "But no matter which avatar we play, we'll never win. We'll only win as our true selves. We have to remember who we are." Theo cupped a handful of water into his hand. "And to do that, we must sacrifice everything we are not."

He brought the water to his right shoulder and poured it over his bicep. The water trickled down his skin, dissolving what was left of the bars, as if they were merely painted on with ink.

He cupped another scoop of the green liquid and washed away the remainder of the markings, watching the water turn black as it rinsed him clean and dripped into the river.

Annelee leaned over and began washing her arm. "I sacrifice everything I am not," she said, "in order to remember who I truly am."

The liquid changed from green to black as it ran down her skin and erased her markings. She pointed as it dripped into the river. "Look!"

As the drops hit the surface, the color transformed into a deep blood-red.

"Surrender," Theo whispered. "Red. We did it."

The color rippled outward, tinging the entire river with a deep shade of crimson.

"Yes, you did!" a familiar voice said behind them.

Theo and Annelee turned to see Sebastian. He blinked his big green eyes, then waddled toward them. "Well done, Dream Travelers." He peered into the river. "There are many legends about red waters ... Stories of people who've drowned in red lakes ... And another story about a mystic teacher who made a very great sacrifice. He invited his followers to drink red waters in remembrance of all that he had taught them."

Sebastian motioned for Theo and Annelee to cup their fingers, then he scooped up water and poured it into their hands.

"As you both now realize, life is a cycle of remembering and forgetting. Which is why it's important to mark the moments we never want to forget." He glanced between the two of them. "I imagine this is one you'll want to remember."

Theo and Annelee exchanged glances, then stared at the liquid in their cupped hands.

"Go on," Sebastian urged. "Drink. And do this in remembrance of the truth."

Annelee brought her hands to her lips. As she took the first sip, her eyes widened. She gulped down the rest.

Theo brought the red water to his lips. As the cool liquid hit his tongue, the world around him vanished from sight.

Light consumed his vision—the purest, brightest light.

A boy's giggle echoed from somewhere inside the radiance.

"Elyon," Theo whispered.

Flashes of color swirled in front of him.

Green mingled with white, then bled into red, which deepened to black, and faded back to white.

"White," he said. "The light—Elyon—is infinite. In him there is no darkness. Nothing can threaten him, and nothing can threaten us because we are the children of Elyon."

"Green," he heard Annelee's voice say. "We are one with that infinite light, because we are the light of the world."

"Black," Theo continued. "But in this world, we are blind to the light. And so our journey is to see the light in the darkness."

"Red," Annelee added. "Surrender is the means of seeing the light."

"And white," Theo concluded. "Love is the evidence of being in the light."

The boy's laughter erupted around and within. Theo touched his chest, feeling the joy of Elyon bubble up inside him and become his own.

The brilliance dimmed, and the riverbank came into focus.

Tears streamed down Annelee's cheeks as she faced Theo. "I remember," she said. "I remember everything."

Heat seared Theo's arm. "Me too," he said as he glanced down at his skin.

A seal of five colors glowed on his arm like a tattoo made of light.

"The Five Seals of Truth!" Annelee touched her own arm where light pulsed beneath her skin. "We've won!" She paused. "But we're still dressed like our avatars."

"You've *almost* won," Sebastian said. "There's still something left to do, and until you do it, you'll remain in your current costumes. You may even find your avatars and their skills useful," he added with a grin.

Theo stared into the red river, his left hand cupping the warm, glowing seal on his arm. Peace washed over him as he allowed his mind and heart to linger on all the memories: his life in Florida, his days in Viren, his old school, his parents, his friends and their adventures in Other Earth. The gentle gurgle of the red waters stirred another memory inside him.

"Blood," he said.

"Huh?" Annelee asked.

Theo pointed to the water. "It looks like blood." He laughed. "That's why Teeleh had to check my hands before I wrote in the Book of History—to make sure there wasn't blood on them." He grabbed Annelee's hand excitedly. "That's it! We have to bleed in the book."

Her eyes widened. "Like when we were in the library at school."

"Exactly. We can use it to portal out of the game, right?" He looked to Sebastian.

The Roush smiled. "Remember, this isn't Other Earth. You're in a game …" He paused, giving Theo the space to fit the final pieces together.

Theo chewed his lip. "And I changed the game …" he murmured. "Blood changes the game. Blood … Red … Surrender …"

And then it clicked.

"I know exactly what we have to do."

"Find a book?" Annelee offered.

Theo grinned. "And rescue the princess …"

"*And* save the Kingdom of Viren." Annelee's smile

widened, and though she still looked like the archer, Theo saw the true Annelee beneath the avatar she played.

"We need to get to the palace," he said.

"But the city is still a two-day ride from here. We'll never make it in time."

He nodded. "Right. We'll never make it as Theo the Savant and Annelee the Archer. But we're not from this world." He raised his eyebrows.

"So?" she asked playfully. "What do you have in mind?"

"We're Dream Travelers. Our words hold great power. And this is just a game."

Sebastian bounced from foot to foot with excitement. "Yes, yes, yes. Your words hold great power. And this"—he spread his wings wide—"is just a game."

"C'mon." Theo grabbed Annelee by the arm and pulled her toward the bridge, then stepped onto the first rickety plank.

"What are we doing?"

"Crossing over into Viren. Close your eyes."

She obeyed. "Now what?"

"We've been in the palace before. Remember?"

"Of course I remember. How could I forget? You threw Marsuuv into the wall with just the sound of your voice."

Theo closed his eyes and took another step onto the

bridge. The boards groaned beneath his feet. "That's where we're going," he said, feeling the power in his words. "When we cross over, we'll not just be in Viren's territory, we'll be standing inside the palace."

They continued across the bridge, eyes closed.

"Farewell, Dream Travelers," Sebastian called to them. His voice sounded distant, as if he were much farther away than the riverbank behind them.

After several cautious blind steps, Theo's foot touched down on a solid surface. He opened his eyes to see Annelee beside him, grinning.

She pointed to the vast vaulted corridor they stood in. "You did it!"

Theo glanced around the palace hall. "*We* did it," he said. "Together."

He lifted his sleeve to see the glowing seal on his right shoulder. "Let's go," he said and took off in the direction of the throne room. "We've got a wedding to attend."

Chapter Eleven

THEO SKIDDED TO A STOP outside the doors of the palace throne room. After sneaking through several of the halls without seeing a single person, he and Annelee had started jogging. After seeing giant vases of red roses and other wedding décor, they'd started sprinting.

Theo panted and wrapped his fingers around the handle of the door that opened into the back of the throne room. "Ready?" he asked Annelee.

She nodded as she removed her bow from her shoulder and nocked an arrow.

He slowly tugged on the handle, peeked his head through, then entered.

Annelee followed silently, weapon poised.

A heavy floral scent greeted them, along with the backs of nearly five hundred people, all dressed in their finest attire, who sat facing the front of the throne room. No one heard or saw them enter.

Theo motioned for Annelee to follow as he crouched low and shuffled behind a giant marble pillar where they could watch the events unfold.

At the front of the room Rosaline stood to the left of her father, King Tyrus. A gown of white lace draped her body. Beside her and to the right of King Tyrus, a giant Shataiki flexed a pair of massive wings, then folded them against his back.

"It's Teeleh," Annelee said in a loud whisper as she lowered her bow. "And Marsuuv." She pointed to the cloaked man who stood beside the giant Shataiki. "We're too late."

King Tyrus's voice carried over the crowd and reached the back of the room.

"Dearly beloved, we are gathered here today to join my daughter, Rosaline, with her betrothed, the future prince of Viren, Teeleh."

Loud shrieks echoed through the vaulted chamber. For the first time, Theo noticed dozens of Shataiki lining either side of the aisle near the front of the room.

"Look." Annelee pointed to a group of people who knelt to the left of the altar. They gazed out at the crowd, wrists bound behind their backs. A Dark Rider stood behind each one.

"Those are the other rebels," she said.

A twinge of familiarity registered in Theo's body

as his eyes locked on one of Marsuuv's Dark Riders. "That's my father—I mean, my avatar's father."

A wave of emotions unlocked inside him. He thought of his real father, his real life, his true identity.

"Theo is Theo," he said to himself. "This is just a game."

Beside him, Annelee said, "And we know how to win. Look, there's the Book of History." She pointed to a pedestal between Rosaline and Teeleh. A book lay open on top of it.

King Tyrus continued. "Immediately following the ceremony, our new prince has invited us to join him at a public execution." The king gestured to the rebels. "His enemies shall be eliminated, along with another group of prisoners, which Marsuuv has reserved for this special occasion."

"The prisoners," Annelee said. "We were trying to save them but—"

"But first ..." King Tyrus's words interrupted her. "Rosaline and Teeleh must make their vows and publicly declare their intent to be wed before the beloved citizens of the Kingdom of Viren. Then, they shall write their bond into this book" —he gestured to the Book of History—"and seal their unity forever."

Annelee shot Theo a look. "Not on my watch." She grasped an arrow in one hand and pointed at the altar with the other. "You get the book. I'll create a distraction."

She handed him the arrow and removed another from her quiver. She dragged the tip across her palm. "Blood ... You said it's the key to winning the game." She nocked the blood-coated arrow and pointed it directly at Teeleh. "It's also poison to Shataiki. I'll cover you, but you'd better run, Dream Traveler. That's one big Shataiki. I'm not sure this will even slow him down."

Theo peered around the other side of the pillar and stared down the center aisle. It was the length of a football field. Maybe longer. King Tyrus continued with the ceremony. "Rosaline and Teeleh, please join hands."

Theo gripped the arrow and sliced open his palm as he'd seen Annelee do. He winced. Hot blood pooled between his fingers.

"Do you still have your journal and quill?" he asked.

"Yeah. Why?"

"Give me the quill."

She placed it in his clean hand, then took her aim once again.

King Tyrus proceeded. "Do you, Rosaline, take Teeleh as your lawfully wedded husband ..."

"Ready?" Annelee asked, her question punctuated with the sound of her bowstring being pulled taut.

"Yes," Theo whispered, then shouted, "Now!"

Nearly every face in the crowd turned at the sound of his voice.

Teeleh snapped his head in Theo's direction. His red, murderous eyes pierced Theo with a threatening stare.

An arrow flew over Theo's head, sailed down the aisle, and sank into the giant Shataiki's shoulder.

The beast roared.

"Run!" Annelee shouted.

Theo's feet pounded the marble floor. Arms pumped at his sides. Hot blood dripped between the fingers of his left hand. In his right, he gripped the quill.

The guests shouted and jumped to their feet as the Shataiki shrieked. Dozens more appeared and swarmed the throne room.

King Tyrus commanded his subjects to remain calm as Marsuuv motioned to his Dark Riders to seize Theo.

But Theo didn't slow. Not even when a Shataiki barreled into him from the left side.

Another tried to grasp his shoulders from behind. It released a pained cry when one of Annelee's blood-tipped arrows struck it.

Theo stumbled, then regained his footing.

Dozens of arrows sailed past his head, each one expertly aimed to hit its target. Shataiki dropped around him, one by one.

He was halfway there when Teeleh flexed his

massive batlike wings. Forty yards away when Marsuuv stepped in front of his master. Thirty yards when a blood-coated arrow struck the cloaked man's chest. Black smoke seeped from the wound and obscured Marsuuv's sinister face.

At ten yards out, Teeleh shrieked and shoved Marsuuv out of the way. The beast bared his yellowed drool-coated fangs and hissed.

An arrow struck Teeleh in his other shoulder.

The giant bat swayed.

"Teeleh!" Rosaline cried.

She rushed toward him, but he shoved her with one of his massive wings and made a final attempt to strike.

Theo clenched his fist to ensure his blood coated each finger. He lunged with his arm and hand outstretched, splayed his fingers, and slammed his palm against the open book.

A gust of air rushed through the room. Shrieks and wails echoed all around as Shataiki cried out in pain.

Theo snatched the book off the pedestal, tucked his body, and rolled across the front of the room to dodge the angry beasts.

Strange mechanical beeps and crackles filled the chamber as he sat upright and flipped through the pages.

"Blood changes everything," he mumbled as he

found the page marked with his own handwriting. "It changes the game, and it's poison to Shataiki—like a virus." Using his bloody fingers, Theo smeared the red liquid over the words he'd written about Teeleh and infected the code book with his blood.

The beast roared.

Theo snapped his head up just in time to see the image of the giant Shataiki flicker. It faded out, then became clear again. Teeleh shook out his wings, lowered his head, and hissed in Theo's direction. A horde of his smaller, flickering minions took up formation behind him.

Theo flipped back several pages and wiped his bloody palm against other lines of text, further corrupting the game's code.

A mechanical shriek bellowed from Teeleh's mouth. The sound faded into a garbled crackle.

One by one, Theo continued to flip through the pages of the book, infecting the lines of code with his blood.

The smaller Shataiki behind Teeleh seized, their images winking in, then out.

Teeleh lunged forward with lumbering steps, swiping with his wings.

One of Annelee's blood-tipped arrows struck him in the ear. He gasped, then roared.

Gripping the quill, Theo flipped to the back of the book and found an empty page. Sucking in a deep breath, he placed the tip of the quill on the paper. Words filled his mind, and Theo knew exactly what to write. He scribbled as fast as he could.

Elyon is the light, in whom there is no darkness.

The light shines in the darkness, and the darkness cannot overcome it.

Theo peered up from the page to see the giant Shataiki sway on his taloned feet. Teeleh froze. His massive chest swelled outward as if it were about to explode.

A crack formed in his flesh.

Light seeped through.

A piercing, crackling tone filled the throne room.

Theo glanced down once more at the open page. The text he'd just written glowed with a piercing light.

He smiled to himself, picked up the quill, and penned one final line.

Game over.

The book in Theo's hands exploded with light.

Teeleh's chest burst open with illumination.

The radiance consumed him, vaporizing him into golden light, as it did with Marsuuv and the other Shataiki.

Silence swept over the crowd, and the light dimmed.

Theo blinked, seeing Rosaline stagger to her feet. He rushed over to her and caught her arm.

When she looked at him, her eyes seemed different than when he'd seen her in Teeleh's castle. They held clarity and horror.

Her hands flew to cover her mouth. "What have I done?"

Theo turned to see King Tyrus. A black film dissipated from the king's eyes like a dense fog lifting. He blinked, then stared at Theo.

"You," he said. "You saved us."

A cheer erupted from somewhere in the crowd, then another.

Tears glistened on Rosaline's cheeks. Her expression shifted to one of relief.

The Dark Riders unbound the rebels' wrists and released them, hugging their former friends from the King's Guard and pleading for their forgiveness.

Annelee barreled into Theo and wrapped her arms around him. "You did it!" She squeezed him. "You did it!"

Theo hugged her back. "*We* did it," he whispered into her ear. "We've won the game!"

Chapter Twelve

THEO AND ANNELEE SAT side by side in the front row of the palace throne room a mere forty-eight hours after having defeated Teeleh. Hundreds of red roses decorated the elaborate space, and the sounds of a lute filled the chamber with its song. Theo smiled and shifted his attention to Rosaline and William— the bride and groom—who stood at the altar, facing one another, both overjoyed to be reunited and finally celebrating their marriage.

Immediately following Teeleh's defeat, Rosaline had pleaded with Theo to help her make her reconciliation with William. Not knowing what his limitations might be now that he and Annelee had conquered the game, Theo had written a short line of text into the code book.

William returns to Viren.

Moments later, William had walked through the doors of the throne room, bloodied, beaten, heartbroken, and more than a little confused at how he'd arrived. But after taking one look at his beloved and seeing the apology on her face, he'd run to her.

A fairytale-worthy reunion followed with many tears from both of them. Theo could only guess at what conversations had taken place between Rosaline and William in the following days, but it didn't matter now.

William glanced out at the crowd, caught Theo's eye, and smiled.

Theo gave a slight nod, then reached over to take Annelee's hand. He interlaced his fingers with hers.

Conrad sat on the other side of Annelee, and Elijah on the other side of him. Liam, who sat beside Theo, leaned over and whispered, "It seems you are familiar with the ways of love after all."

Heat flushed Theo's cheeks, and Liam nudged his shoulder.

"Rosaline," King Tyrus said, "do you take William as your cherished husband, in front of these witnesses, and promise to stay by his side through sickness and health, joy and sorrow, so long as you both shall live?"

"I do."

"And do you, William, take Rosaline as your cherished wife …"

Theo tuned out the voice of the king and glanced around the room to see other familiar faces he'd encountered during his time in Viren. He remembered all of them, regardless of which avatar he'd played when he met them. Even Queen Naomi and her brother, Cain, made an appearance at the royal wedding. Yesterday, Liam shared a rumor he'd heard from one of the other King's Guard: whispers of an alliance between the Kingdoms of Viren and Saxum.

Across the aisle sat the man and woman who'd played the role of Theo's parents during his time as the bard: Reid and Louisa. The woman caught him staring and flashed a warm smile. Theo's breath caught in his throat. He hadn't noticed it before: she looked just like his real mother. When Reid looked his way, he winked at Theo and mouthed the words, "Hey, bud."

Tears prickled Theo's eyes.

As he was playing the game, he hadn't realized they looked like his real parents. Then again, he wouldn't have.

His mom mouthed the words, "We love you, son."

His dad placed a hand over his chest. "We're so proud of you."

A cheer rippled through the crowd. Theo turned to see William, the prince of Viren, kissing his beloved bride.

When he turned back to look at his parents, they were gone.

King Tyrus's voice carried over the crowd. "It is now my great privilege and honor to present to you Sir and Lady Atwood, the prince and princess of the Kingdom of Viren."

Cheering guests jumped from their seats and tossed handfuls of red rose petals into the air.

Annelee pulled Theo to his feet and released a shower of petals around them.

Theo did the same and watched the way they seemed to drift around her in slow motion.

Her wide smile beamed against her tanned skin. She'd tucked a white flower behind her ear. It contrasted with her short black hair and matched the trim of white lace on the crimson-red ballgown she'd borrowed from Rosaline. A teardrop-cut emerald hung on a gold chain around her neck.

Theo felt utterly plain beside her, even in the black suit he'd borrowed from Liam.

He wanted to tell her how incredible she looked, but the words felt inadequate. Instead, he stared into her eyes, not seeing Annelee the Archer but *his* Annelee.

His mind came alive with memories of their adventures in Other Earth, their days together in the library at their old school, and now their wild and impossible journey into the Kingdom of Viren.

He found himself moving toward her, reaching

forward, wrapping his arms around her waist. He leaned in, thinking he'd like to kiss her, perhaps just on the cheek. But her smile drew him in. He couldn't stop staring at it.

He inched his lips toward hers when a hand landed on his shoulder.

"Hello, my friend."

Theo turned to see a familiar and kind face.

"Talya!" Annelee squealed and wrapped the old man in a warm embrace.

He returned the hug, held Theo's gaze from over her shoulder, then winked.

Once he'd released her, Talya reached out a knobby hand to Theo and clasped his forearm in the familiar Viren greeting.

"And what were the two of you just discussing?" Talya asked with raised eyebrows.

Heat filled Theo's cheeks.

Annelee didn't seem to notice his embarrassment.

"It was a beautiful wedding, wasn't it?" Annelee asked, her voice filled with joy.

"Yes," Theo said, eyes once again fixed on her smile. "Beautiful."

"Mmm ..." Talya tapped his staff against the ground. "Indeed."

"What are you doing here?" Theo asked.

"Why, I'm here to send you back, of course," Talya said. "After all, you did win the game."

"Oh, right," Annelee said. A flicker of sadness registered on her face. "I nearly forgot."

"Come," Talya said. "It's time for you to return."

Theo and Annelee waved their good-byes over their shoulders as they followed Talya down the aisle, out of the throne room, and toward the palace exit. He pushed open a pair of massive wooden doors and led them out onto the sprawling green lawn, where a white building surrounded by columns that supported a copper dome glistened in the sunlight.

"A Waystation," Theo said.

He noticed some of the wedding guests had wandered outside, but no one paid any attention to the strange building.

Talya led them inside.

The familiar mechanical hum greeted Theo and Annelee as they entered the Waystation.

"Where are all the computers?" Annelee asked. "The screens are gone."

Theo stepped into the center of the room and spun to take in the scene.

White pillars edged the walls in place of the consoles. Once again, it reminded Theo of the inside of the Jefferson Memorial that he'd seen on his eighth-grade trip to Washington, DC. His eyes landed on the inscription that encircled the room just beneath the dome.

"Remember," he read aloud, eyes tracing the engraved lettering. "Life is a cycle of remembering and forgetting."

Annelee joined him in the center of the room. She pointed to the glowing seal that hung over the door of the charging station. "The Five Seals of Truth." She lifted the delicate sleeve of her ballgown. A matching emblem pulsed with light on her skin.

Talya cleared his throat as he joined them. "The screens and computers are gone because you don't need them anymore. Your time in this game is finished. I do hope you enjoyed this little adventure I orchestrated for you."

Theo and Annelee faced him.

"It was incredible," she said. "An adventure I won't forget."

Talya's bushy white eyebrows darted upward. "Is that so?"

Annelee flashed an uncertain glance at Theo. "I mean, I don't want to forget about this experience. Will I?" She clasped her opposite hand over the marks on her arm. "I don't want to lose the seals again."

Talya smiled as he leaned on his staff. "I assure you, my dear. These seals can never be lost. But, as I once warned young Theo, they can be forgotten."

He reached out a weathered and knobby hand and lifted Theo's sleeve.

"These markings are not merely branded on your arms. They are seared onto your hearts."

The words struck Theo as he recalled hearing them for the first time in Other Earth.

"The ones on your arm will fade with time, as they did before. But the marks on your heart will remain forever. It's rarely our intention to forget moments like these. But life is a cycle of remembering and forgetting." He gestured to the inscription that wrapped the room. "Which is why it is of utmost importance that the two of you help each other to remember."

Annelee stepped closer to Theo until her shoulder brushed his.

"Annelee, from time to time, Theo may need you to remind him that he is, indeed, Theo."

She reached over and grabbed Theo's hand.

"And Theo, likewise, there will be days when you must remind Annelee that she is truly Annelee. You are not the costumes you wear or the avatars you play, in this world or any other. You are the light of the world, one with the true light—Elyon—and the evidence of that truth is love."

Annelee squeezed Theo's hand. He squeezed back.

"Life will lead the two of you on countless adventures—many of them you'll take together. But remember, no matter what world you find yourselves in, no matter what challenges you face, the key is to remember who you truly are."

"Thank you," Theo said. "Thank you for helping us to remember."

Talya dipped his head. "It has been my very great honor." He straightened. "And now it is time."

"What happens next?" Annelee wrapped her fingers tighter around Theo's. "Do we go back into the charging station?"

Talya shook his head. "There is no need. The truth of the seals is inside you." He maneuvered his staff so it leaned against his shoulder, then reached out with both hands and placed two fingers on each of their foreheads.

"Remember," he said.

Pressure formed on Theo's forehead as Talya pushed.

"Remember," he said again, his voice fading.

Brilliant light consumed Theo's vision, then darkness.

He blinked and sat up, allowing his eyes to adjust to the dim but familiar setting.

A soft surface lay beneath him. A dresser sat across from him. A dark TV screen sat on top of that.

He was back in his bedroom in Florida.

Theo's heart raced. He felt around on the bed for his phone.

11:01 p.m.

Mere minutes had passed since he'd last looked at the clock, abandoned his text message to Annelee, and decided to play a game on his PlayStation.

His phone buzzed in his hands.

Theo swiped to unlock the screen and opened a new text message from Annelee.

I just had the strangest dream about you ... At least, I think it was a dream.

A smile pulled at Theo's lips.

He texted back.

It wasn't a dream. It was a game. And it was real.

Theo shifted from foot to foot, staring down a long white airport corridor from the Arrivals pick-up area. He pulled out his phone and opened his messages. It had been hours since Annelee's last text. He glanced at the time in the top left corner of the screen, bit his lip, and shoved the phone back into his pocket.

"Any minute now," he said under his breath.

Three months had passed since a Roush named

Sebastian yanked Theo through his TV screen and into the video game that changed his life. Since their return, not a day had gone by when he and Annelee hadn't talked over text or FaceTime. She'd been nagging her mom for a visit to Theo since the moment he'd invited her. Thankfully, after a few phone calls with Theo's grandmother, Mrs. White finally agreed to an in-person visit over the school break.

A small crowd of people appeared at the other end of the corridor and made their way toward the baggage claim area. Theo scanned the faces, watching them approach.

A laugh danced down the hall.

Theo recognized it.

He stood straighter, smoothed his hands over his shirt, then wiped his sweaty palms on his pants.

His grandmother, who stood beside him, gave him a knowing smile. "I can't wait to meet her."

Annelee's blonde hair glimmered like gold as she passed through the light of a window. She had a pair of sunglasses perched on top of her head, a duffle bag slung over one shoulder, and she wore a sage-green tank top with blue jeans, just as she'd worn inside the Waystations. He knew the color of the shirt would make her eyes look even greener up close.

Annelee laughed again, said something to her mom,

who walked beside her, then looked straight ahead. She stopped, eyes locked on Theo.

An infectious smile spread across her face. She gripped her duffle bag and took off in a sprint, flip-flops slapping the corridor. People stopped and stared, but she didn't care. She closed the distance between her and Theo in seconds and leaped into his arms.

The scent of strawberries and fresh air reached his nose as she wrapped her arms around his neck. He pressed his face into her hair and hugged her back.

A torrent of memories unleashed in his mind.

The forests of Viren.

The hills of Saxum.

Stolen moments in a treehouse, a library, a coliseum.

Whispered words around a campfire.

Life-changing moments beside the Emerald River.

Theo breathed in her scent, then pulled away. Her deep-green eyes sparkled as she smiled.

"Hi, Theo." Then softer she said, "My Theo."

"Theo is Theo," he said with a cheesy grin. He didn't care. Because she didn't care.

He scanned her face, thinking how different she looked from the last time he stood before her. She'd looked like the archer then, short black hair so different from her long blonde waves.

But he would know her anywhere, no matter what

costume she wore or which avatar she played.

Because she was *his* Annelee.

And Theo knew, as long as she remained a part of his life, he could never forget.

THE END

WANT MORE?

Read the first Dream Traveler's Series,
The Dream Traveler's Quest.

Now Available at TedDekker.com:
The Dream Traveler's Game

MORE ADVENTURES AWAIT

Discover the entire
Dekker young reader universe.

WWW.TEDDEKKER.COM

WWW.TEDDEKKER.COM